# Yuletide Guard

## JANE BLYTHE

# Acknowledgments

I'd like to thank everyone who played a part in bringing this story to life. Particularly my mom who is always there to share her thoughts and opinions with me. My wonderful cover designer Amy who did an amazing job with this stunning cover. My fabulous editor Lisa for all the hard work she puts into polishing my work. My awesome team, Sophie, Robyn, and Clayr, without your help I'd never be able to run my street team. And my fantastic street team members who help share my books with every share, comment, and like!

And of course a big thank you to all of you, my readers! Without you I wouldn't be living my dreams of sharing the stories in my head with the world!

# CHAPTER

*One*

December 20th
11:44 A.M.

Samara Patrick parked her car outside her brother's house.

She was simultaneously both happy to be here and dreading going inside.

It wasn't that she didn't love her big brother. She did love Fin, very much, she just always felt so inadequate around him. It was hard to live up to his example, especially given the mistakes she had made. She could live a hundred lifetimes and never make up for that.

Both she and Fin had lived the same rotten childhood, and yet her brother was a successful doctor, married to the woman of his dreams despite the rocky road they had to travel to get there, with a beautiful son who would be two in just a couple of days.

Fin had it all.

And she had ...

Nothing.

Well, not *nothing*. She had a job she adored as a computer expert for a private security firm, she had a small group of friends that she loved and were very important to her, and she had her brother ... kind of. She should be more grateful for what she had and not wish for things that could never be.

Besides, it was Christmas time, a time for happiness and peace and goodwill toward everyone. Her nephew's birthday was Christmas Eve, and two of her best friends were getting married on Christmas Day. She had plenty to keep her busy through the holidays, so she didn't have to think too much about Christmas.

Despite the joy that you were supposed to feel at this time of year, Samara had never had a real Christmas. She'd never had a real Christmas tree, she had never hung a stocking by the fireplace, or left cookies out for Santa, or sat around with her family Christmas morning opening gifts. Growing up, she barely had a family let alone one who put on a big Christmas lunch.

As much as she would like to think that one day she would find her happily ever after, she had resigned herself to the fact that a family wasn't in the cards for her. It wasn't just that part of her believed she didn't deserve it, because she couldn't deny that if a chance at love and happiness came along she wouldn't reach for it with both hands, it was just that she had to accept that not everyone got a happy ending.

Samara climbed out of the car and debated grabbing her coat. She didn't really need it, it would be warm inside, but it had been pouring snow every single day since December 1$^{st}$ and it was absolutely freezing out. At least Ashley would be thrilled. Her best friend Ashley Fallon would become Ashley Watson on Christmas Day when she married her best friend turned lover. Ashley was obsessed with snow and had planned an outdoor wedding. She had been worrying—seemingly unnecessarily—that there wouldn't be any snow fluttering down around them as they said their vows.

She was happy for them, thrilled really, they deserved all the happiness in the world, especially after what they had gone through last Christmas, she just wished that maybe one day she might be the one who was getting ...

No.

She wasn't doing this.

It was Christmas, she would survive it like she always did, and once it was over life could go back to normal.

"Samara."

It wasn't so much hearing her name that had her head snapping around, but the tone of the voice.

Her name had been whispered with a sort of reverence that sent the hairs on the back of her neck standing straight up.

She knew who it was.

Well, not specifically, she didn't know his name, but he had to be the man who had been stalking her for the last five months. He'd been sending emails, and texts, following her on social media with fake accounts, and whenever one was closed down he just started another.

So far, he had never entered her real world.

Until now.

Now he stood before her.

He looked so ordinary, nothing like the image she had built up in her mind.

He had brown hair, cut short, large brown eyes that were currently staring at her like she was about to become his new prized possession. His skin was scarred and mottled like he had suffered from bad acne when he was a teenager, and one of his ears had an unusual scar in it as though it had been ripped apart and sewn back together at some point.

Samara knew how to shoot, but she didn't have a gun on her. Working with a bunch of bodyguards, they had made sure she was trained in self-defense even though she didn't work in the field. She opened her mouth and drew in air, ready to scream as loudly as she could.

"Don't, Samara, please," the man said, pulling back a corner of his coat to expose a gun. "I don't want to shoot anyone. I don't want to hurt anyone. I just want us to be together."

The man said it imploringly like he truly meant it.

She had gotten enough messages from him to know that he was obsessed with her. He believed that she reciprocated his feelings, he believed they were in love and that he would come riding in to carry her off into the sunset.

She just didn't know how he had found her.

Nor did she know what her best move was.

How should she play this, so she walked out of it alive?

Should she pretend that she reciprocated his feelings until she could find a way to run? Should she risk screaming for help and hope that he couldn't really hurt anyone? Her sister-in-law was an FBI agent and was just yards away inside the house, if she screamed then Chloe would surely have Fin call for help while she came out to investigate. But could she risk her stalker hurting or killing her brother's wife?

No.

She couldn't.

Samara preferred the stalker got his hands on her, even if that meant he would kill her rather than risk anyone else getting hurt.

"Please," she said, holding up her hands, palms up, trying to show the man that she didn't pose any threat. Who was she kidding? She didn't pose any real threat to him. She was unarmed, he had a gun and an obsession that had led him to track her down at her brother's house. "Let's just talk about this."

"It's okay." He smiled at her. "I have a place to go. A place I got just for you."

She fought to keep the fear off her face, she didn't want to make him angry. The only thing keeping her alive was that he thought she was in love with him. If he realized that she had no idea who he was or where she had come into contact with him, and that he filled her with fear and anger for intruding on her life, he would lose it.

Samara wasn't sure she had realized the true extent of his obsession until this very moment. Knowing he had prepared a place to take her made her see how thoroughly he had thought this all through. He truly believed that they were in love.

"Let's go," he said. Reaching out, he wrapped a large hand around her arm and tried to pull her along.

Her heart raced in her chest like it was doing what her feet wanted to do but were too afraid to. Her hands were sweaty, and although she knew she shouldn't, she dug her heels in and refused to be moved, she wasn't quite ready to accept this was over yet. Once he had her in the car her chances of surviving dropped dramatically.

"Come on." He yanked her harder. He was bigger than her and was able to pull her along even though she didn't want to go. He began to pull her toward a car a little further down the block, parked just four cars behind hers. He must have been following her.

She had reported every instance of contact he had made with her.

Every email.

Every message.

Every time he tried to connect with her on social media.

But no one cared.

It wasn't a crime to email someone, or follow them on Instagram, or send them a friend request on Facebook.

It wasn't a crime to tell someone you loved them and wanted to spend the rest of your life with them.

Stalking often wasn't taken seriously until it was too late.

And she had just reached the too-late stage.

"Please, just let me stay here," Samara said. "We don't really know each other. Maybe we should spend some time together, get to know each other better before I go with you."

"Silly girl." He laughed. "We know each other. We love each other. And I can't wait for you to see the house I got you as a Christmas gift."

As long as he had the gun—which he kept one hand on while the other dragged her to his car—she had no hope of getting away.

Her eyes darted about nervously, half hoping someone would come and half terrified that someone else would get mixed up in this mess.

Despite his claims they were in love, she didn't even know his name.

He opened the car door for her in an almost gentlemanly manner, and helped her inside, then reached over and did her seatbelt up for her. Again, Samara weighed up her options. Could she make a run for it and hide somewhere before he could fire off a shot at her? Should she play on the fact he loved her and wouldn't want to hurt her? Was it worth the risk knowing he might shoot anyone else who got in his way?

Before she could come to any decisions, he was climbing into the car and turning on the engine.

Then he put the gun down in the compartment in the door.

She knew what she had to do.

As he drove off down the street, he rambled away at her about this house he had supposedly bought for her, but she tuned him out, she didn't care, and the more he acted like he knew her, the more it creeped her out. She wished she knew something about him she could use in retaliation, but she didn't. Every time he contacted her it was from a different name or a different number, she didn't know which one—if any—were the real ones. She didn't even know where she had first met him. He had just turned up in her life one day and hadn't left.

Well, she wasn't letting him have her that easily.

This wasn't going to be pretty, but it was preferable to letting him kidnap her. No one would know where she was so no one would find her, and she wasn't living out the rest of her no doubt short life as his prisoner. As soon as he realized she didn't return his feelings, he would kill her, so if this failed and she died, she was only hastening the inevitable anyway.

The man turned the car onto a busy highway, and as surreptitiously as she could, Samara moved her hand to her seatbelt and unclicked it. Then in one smooth motion, she put her hand on the door handle, pushed the door open, and threw herself out.

12:18 P.M.

"She should have been here twenty minutes ago," Fin Patrick said as he buttered a slice of bread to make his son a sandwich. It was hard to believe that in just a couple of days, Asher, who had been born prematurely after his mother had been shot and gone into labor, was going to be two years old.

"She's probably just running late," his wife Chloe said.

"Samara?" he asked doubtfully. His perfect sister was never late for anything. Being late was something that mere mortals did, and his little sister seemed to think it was necessary to be better than everyone else. Not in some sort of pious manner, because she actually thought she *was* better than everyone else, but because she felt like she had to make up for something she had done when she was a teenager. "Samara isn't late for anything."

"Yeah, okay," Chloe agreed. "But it *is* only a couple of days until Christmas, it's busy everywhere, plus the snow, and she could have gotten held up at work or had car troubles."

All of those things could be true.

None of them did anything to relieve the tension in his gut.

Fin had learned a lot about his gut since becoming a father. Most of the time, he knew what Asher was going to do before he did it. He knew what his son's cries meant, when he was scared, when he was in pain, and when he was just throwing a tantrum because he hadn't gotten his own way.

Right now, his gut was telling him something was wrong.

"What if her stalker managed to find out where she lives?" he asked, voicing his biggest fear. Samara had been living with a stalker for the last five months. The man had sent her dozens of emails and messages and followed her all over social media to the point where Samara had basically shut down her technological world to get away from him.

"As far as we know, he doesn't know where she lives or works. He hasn't had any contact with her outside of her computer," Chloe said, with the same placating tone she had used every time they discussed his sister's stalker.

Like that made things better.

He knew that Chloe wasn't disinterested in what Samara had been going through, in fact, she and her partner had tried to use the FBI's resources to help them track the man down, but stalking cases were hard to prove. Until the stalker upped the ante and made physical contact with the victim, there wasn't a lot that could be done.

"Things can change," he reminded his wife.

"I know they can, and Tom and I will keep working this until we find him, so will everyone at Samara's work, it's just going to take time."

Time his sister might not have.

Chloe came up beside him and ran a comforting hand up and down his arm. Fin turned to thank her for everything she'd done for Samara when he caught a glimpse at what she was wearing. Amusement momentarily pushed away his concerns about his sister as he took in his wife's green elf leggings and oversized sweater with a gingerbread man riding a reindeer on the front. Chloe had an obsession with Christmas clothing. All throughout December she wore it, even at work when she had to be dressed professionally, she usually had Christmas underwear or socks on. He couldn't help but wonder what she was wearing underneath the garish Christmas outfit.

"You wearing anything else Christmassy?" Fin asked with a raised brow in deference to the fact their toddler was in the room, and he didn't want to come right out and ask about his wife's undergarments.

"Snowman panties." Chloe smirked, plastering herself against his side and nibbling at his earlobe.

Fin couldn't prevent the lust that rushed through him.

He and Chloe had lost their first child when he had been born prematurely following a car accident, and the loss had driven a wedge between them that he'd thought could never be mended. Then three Christmases ago, one of Chloe's cases had brought them back together. Following their reconciliation, they'd hit the sheets and Chloe had been wearing a pair of snowman panties that had been both ridiculously tacky and sexy at the same time. The next Christmas she'd bought him a pair of snowman briefs, and it was kind of their tradition to wear them for some Christmas Eve fun that had nothing to do with waiting for Santa Claus.

It looked like Chloe wanted to get started a little early this year.

"Dada, hungry." Asher banged his cup on the tray of his highchair sending milk splashing everywhere and totally ruining the mood.

"Sorry, bud," he said. He was supposed to be making his son lunch, instead he was worrying about his sister and daydreaming about sex with his wife.

"Asher, what a mess," Chloe said, grabbing paper towel and cleaning up the spilled milk. "You have to be careful with your big boy cup." For the last few months, Asher had been obsessed with being a big boy, just mentioning the words was enough to encourage him to be cooperative and try new things. Although Fin was glad that his son was still a long way off from being a big boy, he wasn't ready for Asher to grow up just yet.

Adding a slice of cheese to the bread, he cut the sandwich into triangles, Asher's favorite shape, and delivered it to the highchair. "Here you go, bud," he said. "What do you say?" he prompted when Asher didn't say thank you.

"Tank oo," Asher crowed obediently, grabbing for the sandwich.

Fin smiled and ruffled Asher's brown locks. "You're welcome." Then his gaze fell on the table that was set for three, and his anxiety returned. Samara was half an hour late for lunch, something had happened to her he knew it had.

"Why don't you go check and see if you can see her in the street," Chloe suggested. "I'm sure she's fine and just held up, but if it'll put your mind at ease, then you should go take a look."

"I might do that, be right back." Grabbing his phone from the counter as he went, he dialed Samara's number and headed out into the cold.

He was halfway down the garden path when he saw her car.

It was parked right outside his house.

It was snowing, and snow had already piled up on the top of the car, indicating it had been parked there for a little while.

The phone was still in his hand, and as he got closer to his sister's car, he heard the ringing of her phone.

Fin scanned up and down the street, but there was no sign of Samara.

She was gone.

"Chloe," he screamed as he ran back inside, trying to keep some of the panic from his voice because he didn't want to upset Asher.

"What's wrong?" Chloe asked, meeting him in the living room.

"Samara's car is parked out front but she's not there."

Chloe's brown eyes grew wide, and she immediately picked up her phone. "I'll call it in and get ERT here to check out Samara's car and the surrounding area. We'll get cops out here to start canvassing the neighbors, and Tom and I will go over everything we have on this guy again and see if we can find something we missed before."

He nodded, feeling numb now.

The FBI's evidence response team would find something if there was anything to find. And he trusted his wife and her partner Tom Drake more than anyone else on the planet, but they had already been looking for the stalker for months now without success. Why would they suddenly find something now?

Fin had seen the messages that the stalker had written to Samara; he was utterly obsessed with her. He believed that the two of them were in love and would spend the rest of their lives together.

At worst, Samara hadn't even survived the abduction and was already dead.

At best, she was still alive but a prisoner, which would give them days, weeks, or possibly even months to find her before he killed her.

But she wouldn't survive that time unscathed.

The stalker would more than likely rape her and possibly try to beat her into loving him when he realized that she didn't. And then when he realized he could never make Samara love him, he would kill her.

The numbness was wearing off.

Overwhelming terror was taking its place.

He should have done more to prevent this from happening. He should have forced the cops to take her seriously when she reported the stalking. He should have had one of Samara's colleagues take her on as a client and put a bodyguard on her. He should have done *something*.

"Fin."

He looked up to see Chloe had ended her phone call and was now standing staring at him.

"What?" he asked.

"I might have found her."

"What?" he asked again, a little more forcefully this time.

"An unidentified woman who matches Samara's description was found at the side of the road near here shortly after when Samara was supposed to arrive. Witnesses say she threw herself out of a moving car."

"Unidentified?" He knew that Samara's purse was still inside her car because he'd seen it. If this was Samara then they couldn't use ID to identify her, and if she couldn't give the cops and doctors her name it was because she was too badly hurt.

"She's unconscious," Chloe said.

He had to go to the hospital, find out if this woman was his sister.

"Go." Chloe nodded even though he hadn't said anything aloud. "Hannah is going to watch Asher. Tom and I will meet you there."

Without a word, Fin kissed his wife, grabbed his keys, and left, praying that Samara would be all right. His sister had been through so much and was so busy trying to make up for something that she didn't have to make up for that she hadn't even noticed that her chance at happiness was staring her right in the face. He hoped the stalker hadn't stolen her chance at finding the happily ever after she deserved.

∼

3:03 P.M.

"Mmm," Samara groaned.

Her head beat like a drum, and she felt like she had been dunked in a bucket of ice.

She wanted to open her eyes and find out why she felt so bad, but she also wanted to crawl back into the peaceful slumber that she had been awakened from.

Samara was just rolling back down the hill to blissful unconsciousness when memories flooded her head. Parking her car outside her brother's house, someone calling her name, her stalker, the gun. Being forced to get into his vehicle so she or no one else got shot, the stalker's ramblings about some house he had bought for her and how happy they were going to be together. The fear of being trapped with him for the rest of her life. Jumping from the car, the pain as her body hit the road, and then spiraling into oblivion.

Where was she now?

Had the stalker pulled over to the side of the road and thrown her back into his car?

Had someone else found her and taken her to the hospital?

Her eyes snapped open, and ignoring the pain zigzagging inside her head, she bolted upright.

"Hey, it's all right." A face loomed in front of her, and for a moment, she thought it was her stalker's.

Samara opened her mouth to scream but then her vision cleared and she realized who it was.

"It's okay, Samara, it's me, it's Fin. You're all right, you're in the hospital."

"Fin," she whispered, her voice hoarse.

She was safe.

Alive.

At least for now.

But she knew the stalker wasn't going to leave her alone, he would keep coming back for her until he got her.

Her brother perched on the bed beside her and took one of her ice-cold hands in his warm one. "Was it him?" Fin asked.

She nodded.

It still didn't feel real.

From the moment the first message had come, she had known that eventually, he was going to come crashing into her life at some point, and yet now that he had it felt so removed.

Like this was happening to someone else.

"You're in shock," Fin said, releasing her hand and gently pushing on her shoulders to lean her back against the mattress. He grabbed hold of her blankets and pulled them right up to her chin, tucking them in around her.

Samara nodded absently. He was probably right, shock was keeping her numb for now, but that wouldn't last. Sooner or later, the full force of what had almost happened was going to come crashing down on her.

She wasn't looking forward to that.

"How badly am I hurt?" She kind of hurt all over but nothing other than her head particularly stood out.

"Considering you threw yourself out of a car going forty miles an hour, you're not hurt badly at all. You have a concussion, but other than that just bruises and contusions. Luckily you were wearing long sleeves that mostly protected you, and you didn't really make contact with the road, it looks like you rolled down the grass embankment. You were lucky," Fin said again, a little shakily.

Seeing the fear in her brother's eyes washed away some of the numbness.

Only it wasn't terror about her abduction that seeped in, it was dismay that she was the cause of his fear.

Samara hated for anyone to worry about her.

Especially her brother.

He had worried about her enough for a lifetime.

"I'm okay, Fin," she said, straightening her shoulders and trying to wipe any traces of pain off her face.

"Samara," he said, sounding disappointed. She hated that even more. "You don't have anything to make up for, stop trying to be perfect. This man has been stalking you for months, and then he abducted you. I'm your brother, it's natural I would worry about you, it's not something you have to try to change. You have to find a way to let it go, you're missing out on living your life because you're trying to make amends for something you didn't even do. We both had a rough childhood. You did what you thought you had to."

Rough childhood.

That was putting it mildly.

Fin had no idea.

Still, she forced herself to relax and tried to smile. "Okay, you're right," she told him what she knew he wanted to hear.

Her brother didn't look fooled, but thankfully he let it go. "Chloe and Tom are here. Are you up to answering a few questions?"

Actually, she didn't feel like she was.

Answering questions was going to bring her emotions rushing back, but saying no wasn't an option.

"Sure," she agreed.

"Samara," Fin groaned, apparently sensing the truth, but he smiled at her affectionately and slid his hand under the blankets to hold her hand. "I'm so glad you're here. Even if you drive me crazy sometimes, I couldn't imagine my life without you in it. I want you to still be driving me crazy when we're both old and gray."

Samara felt the same way. Fin had been the only constant in her life, and she couldn't imagine not having him around. "I was so scared, Fin," she admitted. "I was scared he was going to kill me if I did the wrong thing, and I was scared that if I screamed for help, he would kill you or Chloe."

"When you didn't show up for lunch, I knew something was wrong. I'm so thankful you got out alive."

This time at least.

But what about next time?

"I'll go get Chloe and Tom."

She nodded absently. She would answer questions because it was the right thing to do, but all she wanted to do was sleep.

"Hey, Samara, how are you feeling?" her sister-in-law asked as Chloe and Tom followed Fin into the room.

"I'm doing okay," she replied, although she felt like she'd been run over by a truck. "I'm not sure I can tell you anything helpful. I don't know who he is, I don't know his name, and I was too afraid to ask him any questions. I didn't want to make him angry because I was scared he would kill me."

"You did the right thing, Samara," Fin said, reclaiming his grip on her hand. "Everything you did was exactly what you should have because you're still alive."

Fin had to say that because he was her big brother. Samara's gaze moved to Chloe and Tom Drake, but both of them nodded their agreement.

"The most important thing is that you're alive," Tom said. "And you saw him, so you can give us a description, that's more than we had this morning."

She supposed that was true. Still, she wasn't ready to let herself off the hook just yet. "I didn't even get a plate number." She had to be the worst witness on the planet. She had nothing useful for them at all. How could she expect them to find this man if she couldn't give them something to work with? If she'd been able to get the plate number, it would have been as good as a name, and this could have all been over by the end of the day.

"We found the car," Chloe informed her.

"You did?" Samara asked, surprised.

"Witnesses saw you jump and got the plate number of the SUV. We were able to find it, it was stolen, and he must have known we might find it because he dumped it and set it on fire about a mile from where you were found," Tom explained.

"A dead end," she sighed, disappointed.

"Can you run down for us everything that happened from the time you saw him until the time you jumped from the car?" Chloe asked.

For the next fifteen minutes, Samara relayed everything she could remember about the man and what he had said to her during their brief encounter. Chloe or Tom interrupted sporadically to ask a question or clarify something, and she did her best to elaborate or give them the answers they needed. By the time they were done, she was exhausted. She wanted nothing more than to close her eyes and fall into sleep where she didn't have to think, and she didn't have to feel.

"I think that's enough," Fin told his wife and her partner. "She really needs to rest."

Samara smiled gratefully at her brother, between his doctor instincts and big brother protectiveness, it was nice to be loved and cared about like that. Because of the disjointed childhood they'd had—their mom had left when she was three and Fin was six, their father left when she was ten, and they went to live with their grandparents, their grandfather left when she was twelve—they had grown close. They were all each other really had.

"Okay," Chloe agreed. "One more thing though. Samara, we were talking, Fin, Tom, and I, while you were out, and we all think that you're in danger. He probably knows where you live, he knows where Fin and I live, he knows enough about you to make another abduction attempt. We think the safest option is for you to have a bodyguard until we get this guy."

"Don't argue, Samara, please," Fin said, squeezing her hand tightly, conveying his fear. "I don't want to lose you."

That was hard to say no to.

And the truth was that she *was* afraid about him coming after her again.

Maybe having a bodyguard was the right thing.

"Who?" she asked.

"I called Michael. You're going to be spending the night here, and he'll take you either home or to his place in the morning," Fin said, watching her anxiously to find out whether or not she was going to be cooperative with their plan.

She and Michael were great friends, they were the last two of their group of friends who were still single, and they often commiserated about it. It was hard seeing everyone you loved moving on, finding their other half, getting their happily ever afters while you were left behind.

"Samara?" Fin's blue eyes were watching her anxiously.

She hesitated for one more second.

Having a bodyguard would be a huge intrusion on her life. She was used to her own company, the quiet, the solitude, if Michael moved in that would change everything.

But at least she would be safe.

"Okay, Michael can be my new bodyguard."

8:11 P.M.

He had messed up.

He'd scared Samara, and because of that, she could be dead.

Dante Sundry ran his hands through his short brown hair and paced up and down the living room of the house he had bought for Samara. He had chosen it just for her, a beautiful little cabin in the woods where they could be together. The place was small but adorable. It had a porch at the front that ran the width of the building. There was a swing that they could sit on in summer evening, enjoying the breeze off the nearby lake. Inside, there was a large living room with a huge fireplace, which they could sit in front of on cold winter nights, watching the flames dance and listening to the crackling as the logs burned. At the back, there was a cozy kitchen with a large table at the window where they would be able to sit and enjoy meals with the sunlight streaming over them. There was a bedroom with a king-size canopy bed, a bathroom with a Jacuzzi, and a loft bedroom that the children they would one day have would love.

It would all be so perfect.

And he had blown it.

He should have thought things through more carefully. He should have realized that just turning up when she wasn't expecting him would startle her. She had a lot going on right now with her nephew's upcoming birthday and one of her best friend's weddings. He should have known that she wouldn't be ready to leave just yet.

He should have known.

What was wrong with him?

Dante beat his fists against his head until he felt pain.

If he had killed Samara through his own selfish impatience, then he deserved all the pain in the world.

Why was he so stupid?

He was always so stupid.

It didn't matter how many times he told himself to be sensible, to think things through, to be smart, he never was.

It had always been this way.

Ever since he was a small boy, he had been like this, it was why his parents didn't love him, it was why he never had any friends, it was why he was all alone in the world.

All alone except for Samara.

He lived for her, and he would die for her because without her, he was back to being nothing.

She had to be alive.

She had to be.

She had to.

Otherwise, he would shrivel up and perish.

His Samara was so beautiful, so sweet, so pure, she was an angel. That long, silky, jet-black hair, those huge soulful blue eyes, she was perfection.

One day they *would* be together.

It was what they both wanted, he knew that her jumping out of the car today had nothing to do with him. It wasn't because she didn't want to spend the rest of her life with him, it was just because he had scared her by insisting that they do things his way. He was going to have to get a handle on that. He never wanted to scare her again.

Next time would be different.

Next time he would make sure she knew that he understood.

Next time he would make sure that she knew that her brother and her friends were important to him too.

Next time he wouldn't have a gun on him.

That was probably what had scared her the most.

He had only brought it with him in case someone else tried to interfere, someone who didn't understand. He wouldn't let anyone stand in the way of him and Samara being together.

When he went to get her next time, he wouldn't take the gun. Instead, he would wait until she was alone, maybe it would have been better if they had met at her house instead of on the street. That way they would have time to talk, for him to properly tell her about this place, and then he knew that she would be happy to go with him.

It was what she wanted after all.

What they both wanted.

Dante thought it would never happen for him. He thought he was destined to be alone for the rest of his life, and if it wasn't for Samara, he would be.

But now, he had someone to share his life with.

He stopped in front of the Christmas tree.

He had chosen it just for Samara. It was twelve feet tall, reaching all the way to the cabin's roof, he'd had to stand on a ladder to decorate the top half and put the angel on the top branch.

An angel that looked just like his precious Samara.

He couldn't settle for just one angel, between the hundreds of twinkling lights and the sparkling tinsel were dozens more angels. Big ones, small ones, white ones, colored ones, ones with feathery wings, and ones with shiny wings, but the one thing they all had in common was their beauty.

None came close to his Samara.

He couldn't wait to have her here, in his arms, sitting by the fireplace, presents under the tree. His ones for her were already wrapped and sitting there waiting for Christmas morning, they looked lonely, but soon hers for him would be there joining them.

Dante couldn't let the thought that Samara had been killed when she jumped from the car enter his mind. If it did, he wouldn't be able to function, and he had a lot to do.

First, he had to start hitting up hospitals to find out which one Samara was in because she wasn't dead.

She wasn't.

Then he had to choose the right time to go over to her house. Should he wait until after Christmas? Once the two of them were together they weren't going to want to leave one another. He suspected they would be spending most of the winter holed up here together just enjoying each other's company. Part of him thought waiting was the right thing to do, he was pretty sure it was part of what had freaked Samara out today, realizing she was going to miss her nephew's birthday and her friend's wedding. On the other hand, how could he give up spending Christmas morning together here?

He had to go to her right away.

Tomorrow.

Assuming she was in the hospital, she would hopefully be released by then and he could go to her, talk to her, apologize, tell her what he had waited for her here, and then bring her home.

Home.

Dante had never liked that word before now.

He had never had reason to.

Before now, home had always conjured bad memories, feelings of loneliness, pain, anger, fear, but now all that was gone. Now when he thought of home he thought of this place. Of waking up in the morning with Samara at his side, of lazy mornings drinking coffee, of afternoon walks through the woods, of evenings curled up on the couch reading, and of making love before falling asleep with his woman in his arms, and then waking up the next day to do it all over again.

He smiled and reached out a hand to gently touch one of the angels. Soon it would be his angel he was touching.

It almost seemed too good to be true.

But it was true.

He loved Samara, and she loved him, and soon they would be together forever.

Everything here at the cabin was almost ready for her arrival. The cupboards and fridge were stocked, the place was furnished, there were curtains at the windows and throw pillows on the lounge suite. There were paintings on the walls and rugs on the floors. The Christmas tree had pride of place in the living room, and there was a wreath on the front door, but he had more decorating to do. Dante wanted everything to be perfect when Samara came home.

He had hung garlands around the fireplace and on the banister leading up to the loft, but he had more. He wanted to put them every-where, lights too, he wanted this place to be a magical Christmassy wonderland for Samara. He wanted this to be the best Christmas of her life. He wanted this to be the most perfect time for both of them, a new beginning, a chance to start over, a chance to find happiness, a chance to be loved and no longer all alone.

And there was one special thing he had to hang over the front door.

Dante picked up the sprig of mistletoe he had chosen and carried it over to the door, hanging it in pride of place.

What better way to have their first kiss than at the door to their new home, on the first day of the rest of their lives, with this amazing Christmas tradition?

It was so hard to wait, but he wouldn't have to wait long. Samara wasn't dead, he was sure he would feel it if she was. In the morning, he would go to her house, and hopefully by this time tomorrow the two of them would be here together, happy, in love, and ready to spend their first night together.

Smiling, Dante picked up a garland and got busy finishing deco-rating the cabin.

# CHAPTER

*Two*

December 21st
8:29 A.M.

"You ready to go?" Michael Stein asked Samara.

She looked back at him blankly for a moment before her blue eyes cleared and she nodded. "Mmhmm."

"You don't want to stay a few more days?" Samara was a mottled patchwork of black and blue bruises and red scrapes. She was hunched over as though in pain, and she had a concussion. Add to that the fact that her stalker had managed to track her down and had made it clear he wanted her and wasn't shy about coming after her, and Michael thought a couple more days in the hospital was probably a smart idea.

It didn't look like Samara agreed.

The look she shot him suggested he had just asked her to throw herself into a vat of boiling acid that was also full of alligators and sharks.

"No," she said emphatically. "I'm not staying here any longer. It was bad enough spending the night. Fin said I was fine to go home," she added like her brother's word was God.

And to be honest, that wasn't really what her brother had said.

What Fin had *actually* said was that his sister's body had taken a beating, and despite the fact she didn't have any serious injuries, with the number of bruises she had from throwing herself out of a moving car, combined with the psychological shock spending at least another day or two in the hospital would be a good idea.

It was also a safer idea.

With a stalker who had already tried to abduct her once, she was going to be a lot safer in the hospital with a guard at her door than she was in her house where the stalker probably already knew she lived.

Which was why he was here.

Until this man was caught, he was Samara's bodyguard.

That presented its own litany of problems.

His friend and colleague Sawyer Watson thought that he was in love with Samara. Michael wasn't so sure. He didn't allow himself to consider the possibility. It was better to stay friends with her. Friends was safe. Friends meant no one got hurt. He'd hurt enough people in his thirty years, he wasn't going to hurt anyone else. Ever. Even if that meant he spent the rest of his life alone.

Living in Samara's house wasn't going to be easy.

Being so close to her, seeing her every day, and spending so much time together. Could he keep the feelings he wouldn't acknowledge locked tightly away?

He prayed he could.

"All right then, let's get you home and into bed," he said. If Samara insisted on returning home, then they may as well get there quickly so she could get some more rest. She needed to rest to recover in case the stalker came after her again, she needed to be one hundred percent or as close to it as possible. He would lay down his life rather than let anything happen to Samara, but he was a bodyguard not God, and no one could guarantee her safety.

"Thanks, Mike." She offered him a small smile. Samara didn't smile often, but when she did it transformed her. Her large blue eyes got a sparkle in them, and her face relaxed, she looked beautiful. Stunning really. He could stare at her forever. It didn't look like his plan to pretend he wasn't desperately in love with her was going to last very long.

"No need for thanks," he said briskly, picking up her bags and intending to head out to the car, but Samara reached out and caught his hand, stopping him.

"Of course, I need to thank you," she contradicted. "It's a couple of days before Christmas, you're best man in Sawyer and Ashley's wedding, and you have to give up your life for who knows how long to come and stay with me. That definitely deserves a thank you. Actually, it deserves a whole lot more, I don't know how I'm going to repay you." By the time she finished talking, her eyes were looking watery.

Tears were the last thing he wanted.

Michael hated to see Samara sad. If it was possible, he would take away all her pain and fears, and the feelings of inadequacy that he knew weighed her down. He didn't like knowing that she was suffering and walking around beating herself up over her past.

"Hey," he curled his fingers around hers and squeezed, "no thanks necessary. Seriously, Samara. We're friends, there is nowhere else I'd rather be."

His words seemed to reassure her, and she relaxed, her eyes clearing. She didn't release her hold on his hand, but she did smile again. "I guess it'll be fun having a roommate for a while, I haven't lived with anyone since I was seventeen."

He hadn't lived with anyone in a long time either.

Not since his life fell apart.

Michael faked a smile he didn't feel. "We're going to have fun like we always do when we hang out." He and Samara worked together and spent a lot of time together. They were the only ones of their group of friends who weren't married, so by default, they usually ended up together when they all hung out. He knew that Samara didn't like Christmas, and he was certainly no longer a fan of the holiday that was all about love and happiness and family, so it would be nice not to spend it alone. Hopefully, they could commiserate together and help each other through the trauma that was Christmas and all its happy families.

"Yeah, we are. I'm glad it's you staying with me." Her smile lingered for a moment longer before fading away, her usual serious blue gaze returned, and she pulled her hand out of his. "So, we're hoping that he's going to come after me there?" she asked, all business now.

As much as he hated it, that was indeed the plan.

They were assuming that the stalker knew where Samara lived. If he knew where her brother lived then it made sense he also knew where her house was. Since he had been so close to getting her, only to lose her, they didn't think he would be able to wait long before making a second attempt.

Essentially, Samara was going to be the bait to draw him out.

And Michael hated that.

He wanted to lock Samara away in a safe house and keep her there until this was over.

The only reason he wasn't pushing for that was because they still didn't really have anything on the stalker. Unless they could draw him out, the chances they would figure out his identity were slim. For all they knew, this guy was patient and could wait them out until they eventually let their guards down, left Samara unprotected, and then pounce on her.

Michael was not going to let that happen.

He might not be ready to admit it, but he had already fallen for Samara, even if he wasn't sure he should ever take the risk and do something about it. The thought of her being abducted and eventually killed by her stalker almost stopped his heart.

"Mike?" Samara said, and he realized he hadn't answered her yet.

"Yes. As much as I don't like it. I think it's too dangerous, but I was outvoted."

"With you there, he won't be able to get to me. I'll be safe with you, you won't let him hurt me," Samara said, looking up at him trustingly.

Her simple faith in him touched him in ways it probably shouldn't. Pretending he didn't love her was stupid, he was already in deep. Possibly too deep. But he couldn't let things go any further, he didn't want to hurt her, and he had a bad habit of hurting the people he loved.

"I'll do whatever it takes to keep you safe," he said softly. Before he had even processed what he was doing, he had reached out and brushed his knuckles across her cheek.

Samara's eyes widened in surprise, and she chewed on her lip uncertainly.

Michael dropped his hand letting it hang awkwardly at his side.

This wasn't a good idea.

He was in no place to be dating anyone, and Samara wasn't either. Even aside from the oversized baggage she carried around, she was dealing with an abduction and a stalker.

This was a mistake.

Once they crossed the line from friends to ... more than friends, there was no going back.

Was he ready for that?

Was she?

Could he take that chance?

Would she?

This had to be the worst timing ever.

He was surprised she hadn't gone running and asked for another bodyguard.

But she hadn't.

She was still standing there, watching him with an inscrutable expression on her face.

That was a good thing, right?

She hadn't run.

She was still here.

He wanted to kiss her. He wanted to gather her up in his arms and tell her how terrified he had been when they'd learned what had happened to her. He wanted to tell her that he had feelings for her, he wanted to explain about his past and why they could never be more than friends.

But Michael didn't do any of those things. Now wasn't the time for that. Now was the time to do his job and keep Samara alive. He couldn't cope with another death on his shoulders.

～

9:30 A.M.

.  .  .

It felt weird to unlock her front door and step inside.

Although it had only been about twenty-four hours since she had locked the door and headed out to run errands before going to her brother's for lunch, so much had happened, and so much had changed that to Samara, it felt like an eternity since she had last been home.

As she looked around, she tried to find evidence that the stalker had been here. They didn't know whether he had been inside her home, but he had followed her from here to her brother's house, and if he knew where she lived, then there was a pretty good chance he had broken in here at some point.

Samara shuddered at the thought.

"Are you okay?" Michael asked, obviously noticing the shiver.

Michael was another thing that had changed in the last twenty-four hours. They had been friends for a couple of years now, and she loved hanging out with him, but she had never really thought of them as anything other than friends. She knew they were close, and she liked that, she always enjoyed his company. He was quiet like she was, and she knew he had a dark past just like she did, so she didn't usually feel that rush of inadequacy that she got around the rest of her friends and her brother.

Despite Michael never mentioning feeling anything even remotely romantic for her, earlier at the hospital he had been so tender when he'd brushed his knuckles across her cheek. The affection in his chocolately brown eyes had her all confused.

Did he like her beyond just friendship?

Did she like him beyond just friendship?

This really didn't seem like the right time to be thinking about something like that. Someone wanted her. If the stalker could get his hands on her again, he wouldn't hesitate, Michael was here as her body-guard to keep her safe, and besides, she wasn't even sure if she felt anything romantic for him. She'd never really thought about it before.

If she felt something for him, she was about to find out.

Living together in her house for however long it took for her stalker to be caught, and spending all day every day together, if she had feelings for him she hadn't allowed herself to acknowledge, then it wasn't very likely she would be able to keep them locked away. He *was* pretty cute with his messy brown hair, serious brown eyes, and dimples. And he had a very impressive six-pack from working out at the gym every day. She knew that because they were gym buddies and usually went after work when everyone else went home to their families.

"Samara?" Michael prodded when she didn't answer.

She turned to find him putting the chain on the door and closing all the blinds so that if the stalker was out there, he couldn't see what they were doing.

And just like that, all thoughts of their friendship developing into something more slipped away.

Her life was on the line here.

Her stalker was dangerous and knew a whole lot more about her than she knew about him.

"Someone is watching my house, too, right?" she asked.

"Yes, Brady has got everyone scheduled on a shift to watch your house," Michael confirmed.

Brady Crowley was a thirty-one-year-old ex undercover cop who now ran the private security firm both she and Michael worked for, along with two other ex-cops Ryan Xander and Paige Hood. Samara trusted all three of her bosses and was so grateful that they had pulled everyone at the firm together to help her out. While Ryan and Paige were older, in their fifties, Brady was only a couple of years older than her and married to one of her best friends, Aurora, so they were friends as well as him being her boss. She might only have a small circle, but it was a strong one. Certainly stronger than anything her stalker could throw at her.

"Samara." Michael stood in front of her, his hands hovered above her shoulders for a moment before lightly resting on them, his touch probably more comforting than it should be. "We're in this together, okay? That man will never lay a finger on you ever again."

For some strange reason, when Michael said it, she believed it.

Maybe there was something to this more than friends thing after all.

Whatever, she wasn't going to worry about it right now. Right now, she was just going to enjoy hanging out with her friend and do whatever she could to help find out who was stalking her.

"Thanks, Mike." She smiled at him. She was more grateful for not only his friendship but also his willingness to give up his life to babysit her twenty-four seven. Although she had been told many times she shouldn't, sometimes her past did make her feel less worthy of other people's time and attention than she probably would have if she had grown up with a normal family and never been set down the path that had led to the biggest mistake of her life.

Michael smiled back. "You have to stop thanking me, okay? If things were reversed, you'd do the same for me."

That was true.

She would, in a heartbeat.

She would do anything for any one of the people she loved.

"I'll try, but I can't guarantee anything," she joked. She nodded at his bags, which he'd set on the floor by the door. "There are three spare bedrooms upstairs, you can choose whichever one you like, and the bathroom is all yours because my room has an ensuite."

Even though she lived alone, she had bought a large family home because it felt so normal, and she wanted to do some things that normal people did for a change. Living in a nice big family home, with a large yard, in the suburbs, on a beautiful tree-lined street seemed about as normal as you could get.

At least on the outside.

On the inside, she lived alone and kind of rattled around the large house. She never used the formal lounge room or dining room, she basically lived in the kitchen and sunroom at the back of the house. There was a small round table, a couch, and a TV she never watched, that was where she sat and ate her heat in the microwave dinner for ones and tended to her bonsai trees. The rest of the house was furnished, but it looked like what it was, the furniture that had been used to stage the house when she'd bought it. The maid who came once a week to clean her house kept it spotless, but she wasn't allowed to clean the kitchen because that was Samara's own little den, and she didn't like having anyone else in it. It was going to be weird letting Michael in. Maybe while he was staying here, they would use the rest of the house instead.

"All right, I'll go put my things away and then we can have break-fast," Michael said, gathering the three bags he'd brought with him. He walked to the bottom of the stairs then paused and looked back at her. "You sure you're okay?"

Her head felt a little foggy, kind of like when you were all stuffed up with a cold, and she definitely ached all over from slamming into the ground as she jumped from her stalker's car, but other than that, she was actually feeling better than she would have thought, all things considered. "I'm fine, no need to worry," she said quickly. The idea of anyone worrying about her made her uncomfortable, and she wanted to brush it away as quickly as she could.

Michael nodded once like he didn't really believe her but didn't want to push it and headed upstairs to unpack.

Samara was glad that he had let it to, just like she was glad he hadn't addressed the fact that although it was only four days until Christmas, there wasn't a single decoration in her house. There was no wreath on her front door, lights framing her house or Christmas scene in her front yard. No garlands circled her banisters, no brightly colored paper chains hung around her windows or stockings by the fireplace, and there was no Christmas tree twinkling merrily in the corner.

Her celebrations of the holidays only went so far as politely attending friends and her family's Christmas get-togethers. But here in her home, she pretended the holiday didn't exist. She pretended that she hadn't wished practically her whole life that one day someone would care enough to give her the Christmas of her dreams. She pretended that she hated Christmas and didn't want to celebrate it. She pretended that the joy and excitement of others as they prepared for a fun-filled time with loved ones didn't mean anything to her. She pretended that Christmas wasn't important.

She was so tired of pretending.

~

11:54 A.M.

Ashley Fallon—soon to be Watson when she married her fiancé on Christmas morning—pulled her car into her friend Samara's driveway.

She saw Brady Crowley sitting in a car parked on the other side of the street. She knew he was armed as was Michael who would be staying with Samara until they caught her stalker.

This whole thing gave her a horrible sense of déjà vu.

It was way too similar to what she had been going through this time twelve months ago.

She knew exactly what Samara was going through. While the circumstances of how they ended up with someone after them were different, the end result was the same. Trapped inside, unable to live your life, with a twenty-four hour a day guard glued to your side, unsure if you were still going to be alive when the sun rose on the following morning. Ashley just prayed that things didn't drag on as long as they had for her, and that Samara's stalker was found and apprehended within the next couple of days.

"You want to go say hi to your guy before we go in?" Ashley asked her friend Aurora as she turned off the engine.

Aurora looked conflicted for a moment but then shook her head, sending her long brown hair tumbling over her shoulders. "No, if the stalker is here, I don't want to tip him off that the house is being watched. If he knows he might not be brave enough to make another attempt, and if this doesn't work and Samara being bait doesn't lead the cops to the stalker, then who knows when this will be over."

"Probably for the best," she agreed as they both climbed out. "I'll carry the gift, you grab the pizza," she told her friend. Aurora was six months pregnant and shouldn't be carrying heavy things, and what they had for Samara was definitely heavy.

As they walked up the path, Ashley could feel eyes on her.

They were being watched.

And she was pretty sure it wasn't by Samara's stalker.

"Your husband is watching you like a hawk," she said to Aurora.

"You know Brady, and he's been even more protective since we found out we were having a baby." The love in her voice when Aurora spoke of her husband and soon-to-be new little bundle of joy filled Ashley with a deep longing. She couldn't wait until she married her best friend turned fiancé, and they were getting ready to welcome their baby into the world.

"Do you and Sawyer want to have kids right away or wait?" Aurora asked.

"We haven't talked about it, but ..." she trailed off, thinking that they would have this conversation when they both got home tonight.

"But *you* want to." Aurora grinned.

"Maybe." She smiled back, ringing the doorbell. She had a key to Samara's house, but she didn't want to risk herself or Aurora accidentally getting shot if they startled Michael who would be on high alert for anything out of the ordinary. They all knew—aside from possibly Michael and Samara—that the two of them were the perfect couple. Last year when her life had been on the line and Sawyer had been the one tasked with keeping her alive, they had fallen in love, and now they were almost ready to start their lives together. Maybe spending all this time together would be the wakeup call Samara and Michael needed, and who knows, maybe this time next year it would be their wedding they'd be about to celebrate.

"Hi," Michael said as he opened the door, scanning the street behind them before closing it.

"Everything going okay?" Ashley asked.

"So far no signs of him, but it's early yet, I'm hoping he might try to make his move tonight." Michael said the words, but he looked conflicted, and Ashley got it. He wanted the stalker caught so that Samara would be safe, but at the same time, he knew that this was a risky game they were playing. One wrong move and Samara and anyone who got in the stalker's way could be dead.

"Where is Samara?" Aurora asked, scanning the empty foyer, empty lounge room to their right, and dining room to their left.

"Kitchen," Michael answered shortly.

"How's she doing?" Ashley asked. She knew what a huge shock this had to be for Samara. Ashley still remembered every single second of the attack that left her the sole survivor of a serial killer.

"As well as can be expected," Michael replied. "She's holding it together, and I think as much as she knows it's necessary, she wishes she wasn't the center of all this fuss."

That sounded like Samara.

If her friend could have her way, Ashley believed she would make herself blend into the background, become invisible, so no one paid any attention to her. She thought it was what she deserved, it was what her childhood had led her to believe. Some days, Ashley wished she could shake some sense into Samara. But sometimes you couldn't help the way you felt, and she also knew that Samara's feelings were so ingrained and had been there for so long, it was going to be hard for her to see the faulty logic behind them.

"She can speak for herself you know," Samara said, appearing in the foyer behind them. She was dressed in baggy sweats, and she stood as though in pain, which given she'd jumped from a car going forty miles an hour it was no wonder.

"We brought you lunch." Aurora held up the pizza.

"And an early Christmas gift," Ashley added, holding up the large red and white striped box. She'd never been to Samara's house around the holidays before and was surprised that there wasn't a single decoration up. She loved Christmas, and snow, particularly snowmen, and her and Sawyer's house looked like a snowman hotel. She'd known that her friend didn't like the holidays, but she hadn't thought it was this bad. It made her feel so sad that Samara couldn't feel even a little of the joy and excitement that most felt around the holidays.

"You guys didn't have to do that," Samara said, but her face softened, and Ashley could see that she was touched.

"Actually, we did. Last year when I was in pretty much the same place you are now, you two were there for me, which helped so much. So now we're here for you, and what better way to cheer you up than a Christmas present?"

"Thank you, that's so sweet." Samara smiled and pointed to the living room. "Why don't we go sit down. Mike, maybe you can let us have some girl time?"

"Sure, I'll go call Chloe and Tom, see if they've managed to find anything."

Once Michael had gone into the dining room and closed the door, the three of them went into the lounge and sat down. "We hope you like it," Ashley said as she passed Samara the box.

"I know whatever it is I'll love it because it's from you two." Samara undid the large green bow and lifted off the lid, her eyes lighting up when she saw what it was. "Oh, it's gorgeous. It's a Purple Japanese Maple. I don't have one of these, it's going to be such an amazing addition to my collection. I can't wait to start working on it," Samara gushed.

"We took photos of your collection," Aurora explained. "Took them to the garden center and asked for the name of a bonsai specialist. He looked at what you had and thought you'd like this one."

"I do, thank you so much." Samara set the box down and stood and threw her arms around them both in an uncharacteristic display of affection.

Ashley tightened her hold on her friend. "You're welcome. We know how much you love growing your bonsai plants and how good you are at it, they're amazing, and I can't wait to see how you grow this one." Samara's reaction was exactly what she and Aurora had been hoping for when they chose this as a Christmas gift, and she was so pleased they had decided to give it to Samara early. She wished she could fix all her friend's problems this easily.

"You two are the very best friends." Samara sat back, her cheeks lightly tinted with pink as though she were embarrassed to have been so forward when she was usually so carefully restrained. They'd been friends for years now, and although they always had fun together, Samara was so hard to get close to, she didn't let anyone in. Ashley hoped one day they could change that.

"So," she said, opening the pizza box and taking a slice, "Savannah is baking the wedding cake because, well, she's amazing, but we need to make some little marshmallow snowmen, I was going to use them as place card holders for the tables."

"Oh, that's adorable." Samara beamed.

"And predictable, you and your snowmen." Aurora laughed.

"Why marshmallow ones?" Samara asked.

Ashley smiled at the memory. "Last year I made marshmallow snowmen because Sawyer and I were going to drink hot chocolate and have a Christmas movie marathon, only then I found out that he'd been in love with me practically since we met. Everything blew up and then got crazy, and after it all, he made me marshmallow snowmen and asked me to move in with him. It just seemed like the perfect thing to incorporate into the wedding."

"It's perfect," Samara whispered with a wistful air.

Although Ashley had never seen Samara date anyone in the years they'd been friends, it was clear that even though she might pretend she was happy being alone, she wasn't. She wanted someone to share her life with, and whether Samara liked Christmas or not, she hoped that this holiday season Santa Claus would bring Samara exactly what she needed —someone to love her.

~

2:41 P.M.

He was furious.

More than furious.

What was the angriest a person could be?

Whatever it was, it had to be what he was feeling right now.

Dante almost couldn't function. He wanted to throw his head back and scream until he lost his voice. He wanted to slam his fists into the wall until they were a bruised and bloody mess just to try to feel something else besides blinding rage.

He had to do something.

He couldn't go on like this.

If he didn't find a way to let out some of the anger that was bubbling and festering inside him, then he was going to explode.

And that wouldn't be a good thing.

So, what was he going to do?

Dante curled his fingers into his hair and squeezed until pain spiked through his scalp. It wasn't enough. He was vibrating with anger. It pulsed through him relentlessly, consuming him, filling him up, ready to come gushing out any second now.

"Argh," he screamed, shaking his head as though he could physically relieve it of the fury burning inside it.

People passing by him on the sidewalk slowed down, giving him strange looks, and he realized that he was making a spectacle of himself.

Dropping his hands, he mumbled, "Headache."

He had to pull it together before he ruined things more than he already had. If he'd been smarter yesterday, then he and Samara would already be at their new home. Instead, she had arrived home this morning with a man. Dante knew who the man was, Michael Stein, one of the bodyguards who worked at the same firm that Samara did. He had looked into every single person in her life so he had recognized the man immediately.

He had planned the day out so perfectly.

He had been up early and driven to Samara's house to wait for her to come home. He'd brought flowers and her favorite chocolates and had been all ready to apologize for messing up the previous day. He had envisioned her forgiving him and explaining why she had been so scared she had jumped out of his car. He'd thought she would throw her arms around him, thank him for not giving up on her, and then he'd put her in his car and drive her out to the house he had bought for her. They'd kiss under the mistletoe and sit by the fire talking and laughing and drinking hot chocolate. Then they'd fall into bed together and make beautiful love.

It all would have been so incredibly magical.

But how could any of that happen so long as that man was staying with Samara?

He was keeping Samara from him.

That was unacceptable.

He would not let anyone get in the way of him and Samara being together. They were supposed to be together. Samara was the other half of his heart, without her he felt like one of those heart charms where you kept one half and gave the other to someone else. Samara was that someone, and he needed her. She needed him too. She needed someone to make her feel loved, who treated her like she was the special princess that she was.

As much as he wanted to storm Samara's house and take her away, he wasn't stupid. As well as putting someone inside her house with her, they had probably put someone outside it as well. They would all have guns, and they would shoot him without a second thought. Even if they didn't and he managed to use a hostage to get inside, the only option would be to kill the bodyguard and any other bodyguards surrounding the house.

Bottom line, doing that would scare Samara, and that he would never do again.

That didn't mean he was going to let them keep the woman he loved.

Oh no.

He was going to get Samara, and they were going to live happily ever after. Their very own fairytale.

So, he had a plan.

He was just a couple of streets over from Samara's house, at a small shopping strip. There were lots of people about, attending lunches to celebrate the season or doing some last-minute Christmas shopping.

He didn't want to do this, but they had left him no choice.

*They* were responsible for what was going to happen next.

If they hadn't put him in this position, then he would never even be contemplating what he was about to do.

Dante scanned the busy mall, searching for just the right candidate. He didn't want a young mother, that would make things complicated, and he didn't want any men who were bigger and stronger than he was, he wanted to send a message, he didn't want to get hurt. His gaze fell on an elderly couple. They were walking hand in hand, and in their free hands, both carried at least half a dozen brightly colored bags. They'd probably been out buying gifts for their grandchildren. They were perfect.

He waited until they walked past him and then he started to follow, keeping well enough back that they wouldn't notice him, he would just blend into the happy Christmas spirit filled throng. They turned the corner and headed toward the underground parking garage. Could he get any luckier?

He smiled as he followed them, pulling out his keys, not because his car was parked here, it wasn't, it was parked at the other end of the strip mall, but because it made him blend in, he looked like he was heading to his car just like the elderly couple.

The garage wasn't large, and the couple headed to a back corner.

Dante looked around, making sure there was no one else about. He certainly didn't want to be interrupted while he was right in the middle of things.

Pulling his wallet from his pocket, he ran after them. "Excuse me," he called out.

They both stopped and turned, apprehension in their wrinkled faces as they saw someone running toward them. "Yes?" the man asked, moving slightly forward so he partially blocked his wife. That was sweet —pointless but sweet—and it was exactly how he felt about Samara. He would protect her with his very last breath, she was the reason he was doing this, so they could be together.

"Is this your wallet?" he asked, holding it up. "I found it just over by the entrance." He pointed over his shoulder. "And I saw you and wondered if it was yours."

"Oh." The man smiled and let go of his wife's hand so he could pat his pocket, pulling out his wallet. "Got mine, must be someone else's, but thank you."

"You're welcome. Maybe I should take it to the nearest store," he said thoughtfully. "They might come back looking for it, but I don't want to just leave it where I found it in case someone less scrupulous finds it."

"Probably a good idea," the old woman said, smiling at him, at ease now that they thought he wasn't a threat.

They were wrong.

"Sorry to have bothered you," he said, giving a falsely apologetic smile back at the couple.

"No problem, son. Merry Christmas," the old man said.

"Merry Christmas," he returned.

Dante turned as if to walk away, the couple turned to head to their car, and then he turned back and struck.

The elderly couple was no match for him, and he had gone after the husband first, knifing him in the back and then the wife through the chest as she turned in horrified surprise before either of them could scream for help or fight back.

He couldn't stop.

All the pent-up anger he had from not being able to get to Samara came pouring out with each strike of the knife.

Up and down.

Up and down.

Dante lost all track of time.

His surroundings became one large blur.

All he saw was Samara's face.

Up and down.

Up and down.

Blood was everywhere.

It pooled around him. It splattered him from head to foot.

He knew they were dead, but he couldn't stop.

Up and down.

Up and down.

Dante was breathing heavily by the time he finally stopped, holding the knife still, poised above the messy pulp of flesh that had at one time been a body. It was done, they were dead, his message was as clear as he could possibly make it.

Dropping the knife on the ground beside the old couple, Dante looked down at himself. He was drenched in blood so couldn't go walking back to his car like this, he'd be a magnet for the cops.

The couple's car.

They certainly wouldn't be needing it.

Flipping the mangled body of the man over, he felt about in his pockets until he found the keys, then pressed the button, and a car a couple of yards down from where they were flashed its lights.

By the time he was driving out of the parking lot, Dante had already forgotten about the couple he had just murdered, instead, he imagined how the rest of the day would play out. The cops would get his message, they would realize that keeping Samara from him was a mistake, and soon the two of them would be together.

～

3:13 P.M.

. . .

"I am not looking forward to telling Fin about this," Chloe said as she stared down at the bodies before her.

"Probably going to go better than telling Michael," her partner, Tom Drake, said, his gaze also fixed on the bodies on the ground.

She couldn't disagree with that.

Her husband was going to be terrified when he found out what was going on, but telling Michael, who they all knew liked Samara as more than just a friend even if he wouldn't admit it, might really be worse. She hoped that he didn't let his emotions get the best of him. He was Samara's bodyguard, whether or not she lived through this was in part going to be up to him.

The rest was up to her and Tom.

"He lost it," she said, "maybe we'll get lucky and he nicked himself and some of this blood is his."

There was a lot of blood. This was possibly the messiest, bloodiest crime scene she had ever attended. It was a little disconcerting. She kept staring at it, it had spread into a large puddle, and for some reason, Chloe kept expecting it to continue to grow until it consumed the parking garage and everything in it.

"If he's in the system," Tom said.

Chloe looked at him, surprised. "You don't think he's in the system?" It was hard to believe that someone who had done this hadn't committed other crimes in their past.

"No, I don't."

"You think this is his first murder?"

"This was a frenzied mess, it looks spur of the moment, he didn't plan it through properly."

"He had a knife on him," Chloe reminded her partner.

"He did," Tom acknowledged. "But did he have a knife on him because he planned to kill this couple, or did he have a knife on him for some other reason?"

"You think he had the knife to use in the abduction?"

"I think he planned to take a second shot at grabbing Samara but got spooked. Maybe he saw her arrive with Michael, maybe he saw someone in a car watching the house, but I think that was the goal. This," Tom waved his hand at the pool of blood and the two people lying in it, "was a temper tantrum. He was angry that we were getting in the way of him getting what he wanted so he decided to teach us a lesson."

From the mangled bodies of the elderly couple who Samara's stalker had slaughtered, her partner could be right. "How do you think he got them? There were two of them to his one. I know they're older than he is, but still, he managed to overpower them without either of them being able to fight back or even scream for help."

"He probably had a ruse, got them to lower their guard, and then when they no longer viewed him as a threat, he pounced."

Without getting too close—crime scene hadn't finished going through everything in the parking garage, and she didn't want to disturb anything—Chloe knelt at the edge of the puddle of blood. "This was overkill."

"It's an expression of his rage."

It was.

And this man was full of rage.

Chloe didn't even want to think about what would happen to her sister-in-law if this man ever got his hands on Samara.

But she also didn't want to think about what would happen if he didn't get his hands on Samara.

The stalker had made his intentions clear.

Either he got what he wanted, or he was going to keep on killing.

As if reading her mind, Tom said, "I don't know what we're going to do about his threat."

She shifted her gaze from the bodies to the writing scrawled in the blood.

The stalker had left them a message. If they didn't hand over Samara to him by tomorrow, then he was going to kill again. There was no way they would give him what he wanted, but if he was going to pick random strangers off the street to murder, how would they keep people safe?

The best they could hope for was that he had left blood behind, and they got a hit on his DNA. But if Tom was right and this guy wasn't in the system then they had no way to find him. And if they had no way to find him, then they had no way to stop him. And if they had no way to stop him, then how many lives were going to be lost?

Slowly, Chloe stood, her gaze still on the message written in blood. "It doesn't look like our plan is going to work. We hoped he would be so focused on getting Samara that he wouldn't notice that she was protected. But he didn't take the bait. So, what are we going to do now?"

"He's inexperienced," Tom said. "He's already messed up several times. He didn't secure Samara in the car, she escaped, now he has to scramble to try to fix things. But he's out of his element, he doesn't have a plan, he's angry, and that has him making more stupid mistakes."

"It doesn't seem like he made many mistakes with this. He killed them, and then he stole their car and drove off," she said. As far as she could see the stalker had played things well. Even if Tom was right and this was an unplanned spur-of-the-moment decision, it had all played out pretty well.

"Security cameras," Tom said with a smile, pointing at the cameras that were barely visible at the entrance to the parking garage. Trust it to Tom to catch that. He noticed everything which was one of the reasons she loved working with him.

"Good catch. We might be able to get a clear shot of his face."

"If we do, we can get his image up everywhere, and hopefully someone knows him and can turn him in."

"I know you think he might not be in the system, but if we find the car and he doesn't set it on fire like he did last time, then maybe we can get his prints." That gave them two potential opportunities to get something on this guy that could tell them his identity. "Why do you think he stabbed the man only once and the woman dozens of times?"

"Issues with someone. His mother maybe, or a wife or girlfriend, could have something to do with why he fixated on Samara," Tom suggested.

They still didn't know what exactly had led the stalker to Samara.

Back when this had all first started, and Samara had begun receiving messages and emails, and someone following her all over social media to the point that her sister-in-law had had to close all her accounts, she and Tom had interviewed her extensively. It hadn't been an official case, there wasn't anything illegal about contacting someone, but since Samara was her sister-in-law, she and Tom had done everything they could to try to find the person who was stalking her.

Now the case had exploded, with an attempted abduction and now a double homicide, with threats for more murders, as well as the threat to Samara, and they still didn't know anything more about this man. They needed to try to figure out how his life had intersected with Samara's.

"I don't think there's anything else we can do here," Tom said, breaking her concentration. "It's time."

Chloe sighed inwardly. As much as she wanted to put it off, he was right, they had to go and do this. "Are we telling them everything?" she asked.

"I don't think we have any other choice."

"The message, it's going to freak everyone out."

She was dreading having to tell her husband that his sister was in danger.

And not just physical danger.

Knowing what her stalker intended to do—and had already done— was going to crush Samara and put her under enormous amounts of stress. If it were her and she knew that it boiled down to her life or innocent people's, she would want to offer herself up so no one else got hurt because of her. She knew Samara well, and her sister-in-law more than most would want to make the trade.

She just had to pray that she and Tom could find the stalker before Samara made the ultimate sacrifice.

Chloe knew about Fin and Samara's childhood, it had been rough, and it had affected both of them in different ways. Fin had abandonment issues, something that had almost ended their relationship after the loss of their first child. And Samara needed to be perfect in all situations, it was a compulsion for her, and Chloe knew she wouldn't be able to stand back and let them fight her battles for long.

Losing his sister would destroy Fin, and she didn't want anything to hurt her family. She and Tom would work this case as hard as it took to end this before Samara gave in to temptation and gave herself up so no one else would die.

~

4:22 P.M.

Samara loved the quiet beauty and careful cultivation of growing bonsai trees.

Her therapist had been the first one to introduce her to the art of bonsai. At a time when her life had been so far out of her control that she had felt she only had one option left, turning her attention to learning to make something so beautiful had reminded her that beauty did still exist in the world even if it didn't exist in her world. She was a perfectionist and had jumped into learning her new hobby with both feet. Really, it had been more than a hobby, it had been her lifeline.

Learning to use cuttings or other source material, then using a combination of leaf trimming, pruning, wiring, clamping, grafting, defoliation, and deadwood bonsai techniques. It sounded complicated and actually doing it was even more so. Selecting just the right leaves or needles to remove and pruning the branches and trunk and roots perfectly. Wiring branches and trunks to create the form you wanted. Using mechanical devices to shape the branches just so, grafting in new material, and using the techniques needed to simulate age and maturity.

So much went into creating the most magnificent bonsai and that was what she loved about it. It was a way to keep her mind active without having to think of anything beyond caring for the tree. Caring for them meant watering to the requirements of each different type of tree, repotting, regulating the soil composition and fertilization to match each plant. She monitored all of these for each one of her twenty-eight plants every single day.

Of all of her twenty-eight bonsai trees—including the brand new one Aurora and Ashley had given to her earlier today—her favorite was still the first one she'd ever grown. Her little elm tree had pride of place in her yard, it had been a good choice to start out with. You could grow them from seeds or cuttings, and they were a very forgiving plant. Now though, she liked to challenge herself, trying harder techniques and more difficult to grow trees.

She couldn't imagine not having bonsai trees in her life. They were the only thing that relaxed her. They kept her busy and kept her loneliness at bay, they were the one thing in her life that she could do perfectly and didn't have to worry about making mistakes. She liked that, her trees didn't judge her, they didn't expect her to live up to any sort of expectations.

"Hey."

A hand fell on her shoulder, and she jumped a mile.

Spinning around quickly, she knocked over her chair and sent the bag of fertilizer that she had been using toppling to the floor where the bag split open, and fertilizer spilled everywhere.

"Whoa, sorry, I thought you heard me come out."

Samara looked up to Michael's concerned face and forced herself to calm down. She was so jumpy knowing that her stalker was out there and that she was the bait to draw him into a trap. She knew she was safe here with Michael and her colleagues watching her house, but that didn't settle her nerves and take her fear away. It had been a long few months knowing that someone was out there who was obsessed with her, but now seeing how his obsession had grown, she knew he wasn't going to back down until he had her.

But just because she was freaking out internally didn't mean that she had to freak out externally. She had to play this smart because she didn't want Michael or anyone else worrying about her.

"No, I'm sorry," she said, faking a smile and willing her heart to stop racing. "I was just concentrating, getting my new tree settled in, and I didn't hear you come out."

From the look in his eyes Michael didn't believe her, but there was something else in his eyes. Something that was more important than her getting a start when he came outside.

"What's wrong?" Samara asked. A bad feeling was brewing in her stomach, whatever was going on was something big.

"Chloe and Tom are here to talk to you," Michael replied, which wasn't really an answer.

If the FBI agents were here to talk to her and Michael had this look on his face, then they weren't here to tell her that they had identified her stalker and had him in custody. So, what were they here to tell her?

"Fin is here too."

Her brother was here?

He was supposed to be at work.

Fin loved being a doctor, and nothing but an emergency would have him leaving his shift early.

She hated being the emergency.

"Why is Fin here?" she demanded a little more forcefully than she should have. If she wanted to keep people from worrying, she had to keep calm, but knowing that she was about to get bad news made it difficult.

"I think you better go inside, they're in the living room," Michael said. She hated he wasn't going to tell her, but her anger dissipated when he held her hand and squeezed it so tightly it hurt. If Michael was this upset, then this was going to be bad.

Without another protest, she and Michael walked back inside and through to the living room where Fin, Chloe, and Tom were waiting for them. Each of the three had grim looks on their faces, and Samara felt herself start to panic. She didn't want to be here, she wanted to be back outside tending to her trees. That was safe, and from the looks of what she was about to walk in on being in here was far from safe.

Still, she didn't turn around and run.

She made each foot go down in front of the other until she had crossed to the other couch and sunk into it.

When she and Michael were sitting side by side, Samara made herself meet the agents' eyes. "What's going on?" she asked. She didn't want small talk, she just wanted to know the reason for the stifling tension that filled the room.

"We believe that your stalker knows that you're here and that you have protection," Tom explained. "Our plan to use you as bait to draw him out doesn't look like it's going to work."

That was a disappointment, but it wasn't so bad. It meant that this wasn't going to be over any time soon, but if the stalker knew that she was protected then it meant he wasn't going to make another attempt at snatching her.

"So, what's the plan now?" she asked.

Looks were exchanged. It seemed they were trying to decide who would be the one who would break the bad news.

That the stalker knew that she had protection wasn't the bad news.

"Wait, how do you know that the stalker knows that I have a body-guard?" Samara asked.

Chloe leaned forward, her elbows on her knees, the expression on her face trying to be all FBI agent but failing. "He was angry when he realized that getting to you wasn't going to be easy. He killed two people and left us a message, either we hand you over to him or he's going to keep killing," her sister-in-law blurted out in a rush.

"Oh," she said, unable to properly process that information.

"Oh?" Fin demanded, pushing up off the couch and running his fingers through his dark hair making it stand on end. "That's all you have to say?"

"Fin," Chloe warned her husband.

Fin ignored her. "You have a deranged stalker who is so obsessed with you he tried to kidnap you once, and since that failed, he killed two innocent people and is going to keep killing unless we hand you over to him, and all you have to say about it is oh?"

"Back off, Fin," Michael warned, more forcefully than Chloe had, and she could feel the tension rolling off him since he was sitting so close beside her that their thighs were touching.

She should be feeling that same tension, but she didn't.

Samara felt numb.

Two people were dead because of her.

He had threatened to keep killing until she gave herself up.

She had no doubt he would follow through on the threat.

The logical thing to do would be to give the stalker what he wanted.

If she had known this was going to happen, she would never have escaped.

Her mistake had cost two people their lives.

"Excuse me," she said, standing up. She couldn't sit in here with them any longer or she would start feeling things that were going to suffocate her.

"Don't just walk out of here, Samara," Fin growled, trying to grab her as she walked past, but she dodged out of his reach.

"Don't touch her," Michael said, springing to his feet and moving to stand between her and her brother.

"She can't just walk away. She can't hide from this and pretend it isn't happening. We need to figure out a plan. She needs to try to figure out who he is and where she met him," Fin raged.

As if she hadn't been thinking of anything else for months.

If she knew who he was she would have told someone by now.

She had laid awake more nights than she could count, wracking her brain, trying to come up with an answer as to how she had met this man and what she had done to attract his attention.

But the truth was she didn't know.

She didn't know who he was.

She didn't know where she had met him.

She didn't know how to stop him from killing innocent people.

She didn't know anything other than given the choice between her life and someone else's, she would gladly choose to sacrifice her own.

Her life wasn't worth much.

Samara ignored the worried calls of her brother, and Michael, and the agents and ran upstairs to her room, locking the door behind her and sinking down onto her bed.

Her whole life had been one gigantic mess, and she was tired of it.

Maybe turning herself over to her stalker and letting him eventually kill her would give her the peace she so desperately sought.

6:31 P.M.

If she didn't come downstairs soon, he was going to break down her door.

Michael knew it would make Samara mad, but he was getting worried about her. She had been upstairs, locked in her bedroom, ever since she had found out that her stalker had killed two people and threatened to keep killing until he got what he wanted.

Samara.

He was terrified that she was going to give herself to him.

He had no idea how to stop it from happening. Catching the stalker of course, but so far, the man had managed to keep himself out of their sights. Sooner or later—probably sooner rather than later—Samara was going to cave under the pressure. He was responsible for her safety as long as he was her bodyguard, and the only thing he could think of that might convince her to hold on until Tom and Chloe caught her stalker was to show her that although she thought she had made big mistakes in her life, there was always someone who had made bigger ones.

Him.

As much as he didn't want to do this, there wasn't anything he wouldn't do for Samara.

That was it.

She had had long enough to wallow.

Michael was just starting for the stairs when Samara suddenly appeared. Her face was pale, but her eyes weren't red and puffy. As much as she had no doubt felt like crying, she had probably held it in because crying would worry people, and she couldn't cope with anyone worrying about her.

Despite her attempts to the contrary, he knew she was struggling, and he was worried about her. Michael bit his tongue, and instead of asking how she was doing he said, "Dinner's ready. I made your favorite."

She looked behind at the table where he had set up salad, rolls, and risotto. A small smile curved her lips. "Thank you."

He was a little surprised she hadn't pulled out the I don't have an appetite card, but she didn't, just crossed to the table and sat down. "What do you want to drink?"

"Soda, please."

He poured two glasses of soda then joined Samara at the table. Michael wanted to bring up what Tom and Chloe had told them earlier, but he wasn't sure that Samara would respond well to that, and he didn't want her to shut down. Since she had been hiding in her bedroom for over an hour, he'd had plenty of time to think and come up with a plan. He wasn't convinced his plan would work, but he may as well try it out.

"So, I have a deal for you," he ventured.

"Oh?" Samara raised a suspicious eyebrow, her blue eyes clearly radiating that she thought this was some sort of trick.

"It's nothing bad. You don't have to always think the worst," he rebuked gently, aware he was being extremely hypocritical.

"Okay, fair point." Samara nodded and deliberately relaxed her face. "So, what's this deal you want to make?"

"I want you to teach me how to grow bonsai trees."

"Oh," Samara said again, this time her eyes widening in surprise like that was the last thing she had expected him to say. "Why do you want to learn that?"

"Because it's important to you," he said simply.

Samara smiled. "Okay, I can teach you. We can get you your own tree. An elm maybe, they're pretty easy to grow, a good one to learn on, and it's the same one that I grew for my first. Since you're going to be here for a while, I can help you as you learn the basics and we'll get your tree growing." Samara's cheeks had tinted pink and her eyes were glowing as she talked about the hobby she adored. But then abruptly she sobered, the wariness back. "If I'm going to teach you to grow bonsai trees then what do I have to give you?"

"I thought we could make some decorations for Asher's party."

"*Christmas* decorations?"

"Yes, Christmas decorations," he said even though he knew she knew that. Michael knew she hated Christmas, he just hadn't realized she hated it this much until he had walked into her house yesterday and seen that she didn't have a single Christmas decoration anywhere. He wanted to get to the bottom of just why she hated a holiday that almost everyone else loved, but not today. "Your nephew is going to be two. He's going to be so excited with his birthday and Christmas, I bet he'd love it if his favorite aunt brought decorations to his party."

"Way to guilt me into saying yes, Mike." Samara pouted.

"So, is that a yes?"

She sighed, long and deep, but then she nodded. "Yeah, it's a yes. What are we making?"

"Paper chains and strings of popcorn," he said with a grin. Clearing away the dishes and setting them in the sink, he then grabbed the sheets of paper he'd cut up in between cooking and the bowls of popcorn he'd prepared earlier. "I thought we could make red and green paper chains, and some gold and silver ones too. Do you want to dye the popcorn different colors or leave it as it is?"

"Whichever you want," Samara said with an amused smile.

"Let's color it. I bet Asher would love rainbow popcorn strings to put on his tree. I'll color the popcorn. Why don't you start making the paper chains?" He put butter and sugar into a pot and melted it, then added water and vanilla and stirred. Once the mixture was boiling, he turned it down and let it simmer, adding the food coloring once it reached the correct temperature. Pouring it into a bowl of popcorn he stirred until all the pieces were colored and then put the popcorn onto a pan and into the oven to bake for a few minutes.

Before he repeated the process with another color, Michael turned to watch Samara. She was busily taking strip after strip of paper, alternating between red and green, and had already made the chain several feet long. While she wasn't smiling, she looked relaxed and happy to be performing the mindless task, but he didn't want her to be just going through the motions, he wanted her to be enjoying this.

"Want to help me make the next color?" he asked.

"I've never colored popcorn before," Samara replied, looking up.

"That's okay, it's not hard, I'll show you how."

"Okay," Samara said, a little uncertainly as she pushed back from the table and joined him at the stove.

"Put two tablespoons of butter and one cup of sugar in the pot," he instructed. When she had done that, he said, "Just stir it until the butter melts, then we put in three quarters of a cup of water and half a teaspoon of vanilla extract and bring it to the boil. Then we let it simmer until it reaches 238 degrees."

"Are we using a candy thermometer like when you make fudge?"

"Yep," he nodded. "You should make some fudge to take to the party."

"I don't know about that," she said.

"Come on, you make *the best* fudge I have ever tasted." Her cheeks reddened with embarrassment, but she smiled. Michael wished he could make her smile more often. "As soon as it reaches temperature we add the coloring, then we get it into the bowl with the popcorn and cover it. Then we bake it for a few minutes."

"It's boiling," she announced, already reaching for the thermometer and turning the heat on the stove down to let it simmer.

"It sure is. What color do you want to do this time? I did red already."

"Then green I guess. They're the Christmas colors, right?"

Before he let her mood get her down again, he passed her the green. "We still have to do blue, purple, orange, pink, and yellow. Then we'll let the popcorn sit overnight, and we can string it tomorrow. Once we've done it all I'll help you with the paper chains."

Samara cocked her head to the side, looking at him inquisitively. "Why are you so excited about doing this? I know we're friends, and I know you're friends with Fin and Chloe as well, but why are you *so* excited about making Christmas decorations for my nephew's birthday?"

"Because making the paper chains and strings of popcorn, it reminds me of growing up as a kid. Every Christmas Eve, my brother, sister, parents, and I would all sit around laughing and talking as we colored popcorn, strung it up, and made paper chains to hang all around the tree. We'd have Christmas carols playing in the background, and we'd eat Christmas cookies and drink hot chocolate, the Christmas tree would be twinkling, and the fire crackling, and everything was so perfect. Heidi was too young her first Christmas, but ..." he trailed off. Although he knew he needed to remind Samara that she wasn't the only one who had made mistakes and that she didn't have to keep punishing herself for it, actually saying the words was a lot harder than he thought it would have been.

"I'm sorry, Mike." Samara abandoned the stove and put a hand on his arm.

"She would have been ten by now, and we would have been sitting doing this together on Christmas Eve, laughing and talking, and having fun. But she'd not here. Because of me. Samara, you think that just because there was something in your past you wish you could take back means that you have to suffer for it for the rest of your life, but you aren't the only one that wishes they could take something back."

"What happened to Heidi was an accident," Samara reminded him.

Yeah.

An accident.

That was what it had been ruled.

Just an accident.

A tragic accident.

But calling it that didn't change the facts that he had run over his twenty-month-old daughter with his car, killing her instantly.

He had gotten a girl pregnant when they were both in college. At twenty years old, neither of them had loved the other, and their baby hadn't brought them together. Instead, they had decided to co-parent, sharing custody and all decision making when it came to their daughter.

One day he had been dropping Heidi off at her mother's, he'd taken his daughter inside, done the usual handover summary of how she'd slept, and what she'd eaten, and what they'd done, then he'd kissed her cheek, said goodbye and gotten into his car. Only his ex hadn't noticed Heidi follow him out the door. Assuming Heidi was safely inside, he reversed out the driveway, never seeing the toddler until his car hit her.

The case had been investigated, deemed an accident and no charges had been filed, but the knowledge that he had killed his precious baby girl had metaphorically killed him. He had started drinking to try to dull the pain. Having joined the police force about a year before his daughter's death, he had tried to hide his drinking, and for a while he had. But then he'd made a mistake on a case, and someone had died, and that was it. He'd quit, and stopped drinking cold turkey, he'd called up his old friend Brady who had recently taken over a private security firm and taken a job, and for the last few years, he had managed to regain some control over his life.

But that control was always hanging on by a very thin thread.

A thread that could snap at a moment's notice.

"We've all made mistakes, and no one's are bigger than mine," Michael told Samara. "I care about you, I know that finding out what your stalker plans to do makes you want to offer yourself up to him, but don't, Samara. Please. I've already lost one person I loved in the most horrific way possible, I don't want to lose another."

"Love?" Samara echoed, her beautiful blue eyes looking up at him seeking the truth about his feelings for her.

"We've been friends for years now, I care about you a lot," he said, backtracking slightly because the prospect of allowing himself to love another human being with the same depth of love he'd had for his daughter was utterly terrifying and made him want to lose himself in a bottle of scotch.

"Friends, right." Samara nodded, her gaze returning to the stove where the pot had boiled dry. "We better start that one over."

Michael knew he should tell her. Explain to her that what he felt for her went so far beyond friendship that they weren't even in the same stratosphere. Explain the fear of loving another only to lose them. Explain that he was an alcoholic and that he couldn't ever risk himself hurting her.

He should, but he couldn't.

Heidi was dead because of him, and innocent people were dead because of him. How could he risk Samara being hurt because of him?

Friends was safe.

And for his own sanity as well as hers, he had to choose safe.

9:44 P.M.

Beneath him, Ashley's eyes fell closed, and her head tipped back as she fell over the edge into indescribable ecstasy. Between her internal muscles clenching around him and the blissful moan that fell from her lips, Sawyer was also tossed over the edge into ecstasy with a blissful moan of his own.

As he slowly rode down from the high he would never get enough of, he slid out of Ashley and reluctantly left the bed only long enough to toss the condom in the bin in the bathroom, then quickly returned to join his fiancée in bed.

"What?" he asked as he slid back under the covers and snuggled

Ashley close against his side. She was looking at him with an odd expression on her face, and he wondered where her train of thought had gone.

"I was just thinking maybe we won't be needing condoms for much longer," she replied.

It was hard to believe that this was real.

Sawyer had been in love with Ashley basically since they'd met, but she hadn't felt the same way—or even been aware of his feelings—and they had done the friends thing for a while. But now they were engaged, they lived together, and here she was talking about having kids.

"You want to start trying for a baby?" he asked.

"Don't you?" Ashley propped her chin on his chest so she could look at him.

"I do," Sawyer replied. He had wanted a baby, part him and part Ashley, for as long as he could remember. Even more so since his twin sister and her husband had had their first baby in August. From the moment he had held the tiny infant in his hand, he had known how much he wanted to have kids with the woman he loved. "I just wasn't sure that you'd want to start trying so quickly."

"It's not really quickly," Ashley protested. "We've known each other for years, and okay, yeah, we've only been together as a couple since last Christmas but because we were best friends for so long before that, it feels like we've been together forever."

"I can't believe that our wedding is only four days away." The last year had flown by, and it seemed so surreal that in just a couple of days he would finally be getting what he had dreamed about for so long. Between planning the wedding, work, family, friends, and what was going on with Samara, he and Ashley had barely had time to see each other and exchange a few words let alone make love and talk about starting a family.

"I can't believe that this time last year I didn't even know how you felt about me," Ashley said, pressing a kiss to the side of his neck.

"I wish it hadn't all gone down the way it did, but I'm so glad you know now." Just twelve months ago, Sawyer had been convinced that he and Ashley would never stand a chance and had determined to carry the secret of his feelings for her with him to his grave. And now he had it all.

"Me too." Ashley kissed him again, but there was a troubled look on her face now.

"What's wrong?" His hand began to trail up and down her bare back, tracing the length of her spine with his fingertips.

"Everything that happened last year, with my stalker, and you being my bodyguard, and everyone trying to figure out who it was that wanted me dead, it all just feels so similar to what's happening now with Samara."

Because she was plastered against his side, Sawyer felt the shiver rocket through her as she reminisced about the hell she had lived through last year. Ashley had very nearly been the target of a vicious serial killer who didn't like that one of his intended victims had survived and had been determined to correct that mistake.

"But everything worked out okay," he reminded her, pulling her closer, he hated thinking about that just as much as Ashley did.

"It almost didn't."

"But it did. Ash, none of us are going to let that man get to Samara again." Sawyer tried to soothe his fiancée's fears.

"That's not what I'm worried about," Ashley said quietly.

"You're worried she's going to cave under pressure and do what the stalker demanded." Sawyer couldn't deny that he was worried about that too. They all knew about Samara's past and that her need to not let anyone down and her compulsion to be as perfect as it was humanly possible to be could wind up getting her killed.

"I hope Michael is watching her carefully."

"If anyone would be, it's him."

"He can't watch her every second of the day though."

"No, he can't, but he's not the only one keeping an eye on her. All of us are taking shifts watching the house. If she tries to sneak out, then someone will notice."

"I hope you're right." Ashley laid her head down on his chest and rested a hand on his stomach. He picked it up and entwined their fingers.

"Who knows, maybe this is what Samara and Michael need to give them the courage to let go of their fears and see if they could fall in love.

As awful as what happened last year was, it did bring us together." Sawyer lifted their joined hands and kissed the back of Ashley's.

"Maybe. I just wish that there was something I could do for her."

"There is something you can do for Samara," he reminded her. "Exactly what you've *been* doing. Be her friend. Be there to support her. Let her know that you're there for her if she needs anything or if she wants to talk. Be the friend that you've always been for her."

"It doesn't feel like enough, I feel so helpless."

Sawyer kissed the top of her head, he might not like seeing his fiancée worry about not being able to do enough to help one of her friends, but he loved that she cared that much. "What did you want people to do for you this time last year when you were in a similar situation to what Samara is in now?"

"I wanted them to not worry about me too much, and I didn't want to be treated any differently than normal, and I wanted to just hang out with my friends like nothing was wrong."

"Is that what you've been doing for Samara?"

"I guess so."

"Then you're doing enough." He kissed the top of her head again. "Samara is strong, and she has Chloe and Tom working this case as hard as they can, and all of us working round the clock to keep her safe. With Asher's birthday and our wedding, she has plenty to keep her busy and occupied. Just keep doing what you're doing, I know she appreciates it."

"I suppose you're right," Ashley said with a sigh.

"You don't have to sound so happy about it," he teased.

Ashley huffed a small laugh. "Okay, you're right, we have to believe that everything will work out in the end just like it did for me. And if I hadn't lived through that hell then I never would have gotten you. Maybe you're right. Maybe Samara and Michael will get the same happy ending that we did. It is Christmas time after all."

"You ready to go to sleep then?" he asked. The quicker they turned off the light and went to sleep, the quicker it would be tomorrow and one day closer to their wedding.

"Nope." Ashley lifted her head off his chest, a mischievous smile on her face.

"You want a snack?" His fiancée had a thing for late-night snacks.

He couldn't count the number of times in the last year that he had rolled over in bed in the early hours of the morning to find she wasn't there but down in the kitchen eating or preparing a snack.

"Nope," Ashley said as her hand dipped under the covers.

"Oh," he said as her fingers curled around him, and his body instantly responded. He reached down and snagged her hand, if she kept that up it was going to be a pretty one-sided event. Sawyer flipped her onto her back and crushed his mouth to hers, his hand moving between her legs and doing a little stroking of its own.

"No fair." Ashley pouted playfully, squirming beneath him. "You wouldn't let me touch you, but you get to touch me?"

"I guess we can settle on something that satisfies us both." He laughed. Sawyer was just about to reach for the box of condoms in the nightstand drawer when he froze, thinking about what she'd said earlier. "Condom?"

Ashley didn't even hesitate. "I don't think we need one."

"I love you, Ash."

"I love you, too."

As he slid inside his soon-to-be wife, Sawyer couldn't help but think that he was the luckiest guy in the world. In just four days he would be making this gorgeous woman his wife, and who knew, tonight they might be making a baby.

# CHAPTER
*Three*

December 22nd
9:06 A.M.

"How do you know which leaves to trim? Or what roots to cut?"

"Practice," Samara answered as she handed Michael a terracotta pot and a bag of lava rock.

"Will I be able to grow bonsai trees as pretty as yours?"

She smiled despite herself, and the heavy weight of pressure that had been tied to her back when Chloe and Tom had told her that her stalker had killed and was going to keep on killing eased slightly. "Eventually you will."

"Which one is your favorite?" Michael asked as he spread the lava rock over the bottom of the pot.

"The elm tree, it was the first one I grew, so it's always been kind of special to me."

"This one is definitely going to be my favorite." He smiled at her as he set the lava rock down.

The smile was deceiving.

It was meant to pacify her, encourage her to hold it together, and not do anything rash like runoff and hand herself over to her stalker, which had been the point of their conversation last night. Samara had already known that Michael's daughter had died many years ago. She had even known that although it was an accident it was at Michael's hand, but she hadn't known all the details until last night.

He'd told her because he wanted to convince her that he had made bigger mistakes in his life than she had, but he was wrong.

As tragic as it was, Heidi's death was just an accident.

Michael hadn't done anything wrong. He hadn't made a conscious decision to run over his twenty-month-old daughter.

On the other hand, she was one hundred percent responsible for the mistakes she had made.

Their pasts were different, and while both had impacted them and the people they had grown into, that didn't mean that there were any more similarities than that.

Deep down, Michael knew that was true.

That was why he had backtracked last night.

He'd made it sound like he loved her, but then he'd covered, said he just loved her as a friend, and in that moment, Samara had realized that she was disappointed. She wanted Michael to like her. She wanted him to love her like she had never been loved before. She wanted someone to love her, she wanted to matter to someone, to be important to someone, to be cared about and cared for.

Wasn't that what everyone wanted?

It was just looking less and less likely that she would ever get it.

"Samara?"

"Yeah?" She blinked and tried to hide the tears building in her eyes.

"What next?"

This was silly.

She and Michael had never been anything more than friends, so why did it feel like she had just lost a piece of herself?

"Umm, soil next," she said, passing him a bag.

He sprinkled some in and then looked at her expectantly.

"You need to prune the branch at a forty-five-degree angle," she said, pointing to the shears. "Then you put the cutting into the soil, about an inch deep, and water it in."

"That's it?" he asked, following her instructions.

"For now. Once it starts to grow, then we get to work."

"I can't wait to grow ones like these." Michael stood and surveyed her collection, stopping in front of one in particular. "This one looks like a Christmas tree."

"It's a Colorado Blue Spruce," she corrected automatically. It was a lame comeback, Samara knew that because Colorado Blue Spruces were often used as Christmas trees. She just didn't like the thought of having anything Christmassy in her house.

"Let's go back inside, it's cold out," Michael said, taking her hand and leading her from the covered porch back into the sunroom. He guided her to the couch and very gently pushed her down onto it, sitting beside her.

She knew what he was going to say even before he spoke the words.

"Why do you hate Christmas so much, Samara?"

She wanted to ignore him.

Or claim ignorance, pretend that she had no problem with the holiday, but he would know she was lying. If she didn't hate Christmas, then her house would be decorated with twinkly lights, tinsel, and a tree.

"You know why," she muttered helplessly. Couldn't Michael see that she didn't want to talk about this?

"Because of your family," he said.

Samara nodded. "I didn't have a family. Well, not the normal kind anyway. I've never had a real Christmas, not that I can remember at least. Maybe before my mom left, but I was too young."

"You were three when she left, right?"

"I was. I don't remember it, but I know Fin does. He was older, six by then, so he remembers that day. I don't. I don't even remember her. She just left because she didn't want us anymore. She wasn't having an affair or anything, she just didn't want to be a mother. So, she left. My dad wasn't really interested in being a parent, so he mostly left us to ourselves. He never did the whole Christmas thing with us. No tree, decorating, gifts, Santa Claus, or big family dinner, nothing. When he started dating this woman when I was eight, I thought things might be different. I felt left out not having a mother, and I thought it would be nice to have one again. But that wasn't her plan. She had kids of her own and didn't want anymore, so we were sent to live with his parents when she married my dad. I was ten by then. My grandparents were old, and they didn't want to be raising kids again, so they didn't do any of the usual parent things with us. They gave us a house to live in and food on the table, but that was it. My grandfather only lasted two years before he left as well. I guess Christmas just became a symbol of everything that we didn't have that everyone else did, and I don't know," she shrugged, "I just don't like it."

"I'm sorry, Samara. I hate that you grew up never feeling wanted."

"They messed us up pretty good. Fin has abandonment issues which very nearly ruined his relationship with Chloe. And I have ..." she trailed off, not even really sure how to describe it.

"If you could make your perfect Christmas, wipe away all the bad memories and start fresh, what would your Christmas look like?" Michael asked.

The question caught her by surprise, and she had to take a moment to think. Usually, she just avoided thinking about the holiday at all, she didn't try to envision how she would celebrate it if she could. "Umm, I guess, just all the traditional stuff. The things everyone else does."

"Like what specifically?" Michael pushed.

"Well, a wreath on the door and lights all around the roof. A Christmassy display on the front lawn, a Santa in a sleigh, and reindeer. And inside, garlands all around the banister, the doorways strung with lights, and a garland around the fireplace mantle too. Stockings hanging by the fireplace and a Christmas tree in the corner full of lights, tinsel, and decorations that are all special because they mean something to you. Gifts all wrapped in brightly colored paper under the tree, freshly baked homemade cookies and a gingerbread house, hot chocolate in front of the fireplace, Christmas carols playing in the background, leaving milk and cookies out for Santa and carrots for the reindeer, and reading 'Twas the Night Before Christmas before going to bed Christmas Eve. And then on Christmas Day, everyone you love gathers together to have a huge Christmas dinner with more food than anyone could ever eat in just one meal. Oh, and mistletoe, I always kind of liked the idea of that tradition."

All the things she had never done.

It was odd to be twenty-eight and never having celebrated Christmas in your life.

Well, that wasn't exactly true. The last few years, ever since Fin had been with Chloe, she had celebrated with them Christmas Day, but it wasn't a real celebration because she couldn't let it be. Celebrating Christmas was for people who had people to celebrate with, and she didn't. Not really. Because she didn't know how to let go of her past and focus on her future. Every time she thought she did she realized that she was just deluding herself.

"I wish I could give you a Christmas like that," Michael said softly, tearing her out of her thoughts.

Samara wished he could too.

She wished someone could take away everything bad that had ever happened in her life and make it like it never existed.

She wished someone could undo all the damage that had been done so early on in her life that she was afraid it was so ingrained in her very being that it couldn't be undone.

But wishes were just that; wishes.

∼

9:51 A.M.

Michael wished that he could take away Samara's pain and show her just how magical Christmas could be when you celebrated it with people who loved you.

He wished that he could show her that she was special to *him*.

He wished that he could give her the Christmas of her dreams.

He wished he could give her the love she so desperately craved.

If he could, Michael would give her everything she wanted and so much more.

But before he could do any of those things, he had to find a way to let go of his own fears. To bury his inner demons once and for all. And to do that, he had to find a way to forgive himself for his daughter's death.

That he didn't foresee happening.

One event, one moment in time could change everything.

That was what had happened to him.

He had been happy, juggling finishing college and joining the police force with raising a baby had been hard, but he had loved every second of it. Sending Heidi back to her mother every week was hard, and he missed her like crazy, counting down the days until it was back to his week to have her. To make things easier, he and Heidi's mother had hired a nanny so that Heidi had the consistency of one carer while they both balanced their studies and jobs with their daughter.

Sharing custody of Heidi, only getting to have her with him half the time had made him realize that the next time he had a child he wanted it to be with someone he loved so that he didn't have to miss out on one second of that child's life.

If he had to pick someone to be the mother of his next child, it would be someone just like Samara. Caring, kind, compassionate, sweet, caring more about others than they did themselves, the very antithesis of selfish. Samara wasn't just everything he would want in a mother of his children. She was also everything he had ever wanted in a partner.

So why was he letting her get away?

Why wasn't he doing everything within his power to make her his?

At the back of his mind, Michael had always known that he felt something for Samara beyond friendship, but the last few days, realizing what he could have lost if Samara hadn't escaped the stalker had forced him to confront his feelings.

Confronting his feelings had made him realize that he loved her.

He'd never been in love before, but what he felt for Samara was strong. It was like a physical thing that had taken up residence in his heart and poked at him and poked at him, annoyed he wasn't doing anything about it.

Now it was time to decide.

Confess that what he'd said last night was true and that he loved her, or keep quiet and accept that friendship wasn't such a bad thing to have.

The problem with accepting that all he and Samara might ever have was friendship meant accepting the risk that one day he would have to watch Samara move on and have a relationship with another man. Or even worse, watch her never move on and remain alone just because she thought that she had to punish herself for something she hadn't even done wrong.

Samara sighed and stood up, and Michael realized that she had been waiting for him to say more only he'd gotten lost in thought.

"I should really get started wrapping Christmas gifts," Samara said, collecting tape and scissors from a drawer. "I was putting it off, but there are only a few days to go, so I better get it done."

Before he could say anything, she had disappeared up the stairs.

It was time to decide.

And he honestly didn't know which was the best option.

His heart had one opinion, but his head had another.

Life had been so much easier before Heidi's death. It was hard to live and have any trust and confidence in yourself when you had a piece of yourself missing.

He didn't have any gifts to wrap, he'd done that a couple of weeks ago. He was one of those people who usually had his Christmas shopping finished well before Halloween, but there was still some of the colored popcorn leftover from last night so he might as well make another string. He'd hoped to get a little Christmas spirit in Samara by making the popcorn strings and paper chains, but he thought the conversation about mistakes in your past not meaning you had to give up your future had kind of put a dampener on things.

Maybe he could get a second chance at making her like the holiday a little more with the gift wrapping.

"Mike?"

"Yeah?"

"Can you help me with the bags?" Samara called out from upstairs.

"Sure thing." He left the popcorn on the table and took the stairs two at a time. "Whoa, that is a lot of stuff," Michael said when he saw the amount of gift bags she had.

"I might not like Christmas, but it doesn't mean I don't like buying gifts for the people I love," she said with a smile.

That was one of the things he loved the most about her, she was always way more interested in other people than she was herself. It was a great quality to have, except when it made you vulnerable to a violent stalker who would use that against you.

"You're amazing, you know that, don't you?"

Samara's cheeks tinted pink, and her large blue eyes dipped down to look at the floor, a curtain of dark hair falling forward partially obscured her face.

"Don't do that," he rebuked, stepping closer and gently grasping her chin, tilting her face up, and tucking her hair behind her ear. "Don't pretend you aren't amazing and very special. You think that feeling so abandoned and unwanted that you attempted suicide means you have to try to make up for that by being perfect, but you're wrong. I'm not a psychologist, but I'm pretty sure that was a cry for help, a cry for someone to care. Well, I care, Samara. *I* care."

He had intended that to touch her, make her see herself as he saw her, but instead, her eyes grew watery and her gaze dipped again, refusing to meet his.

"What's wrong?" Was she just upset about him mentioning her suicide attempt when she was thirteen or was there more to it than that?

"I ... it was ... there was more ..." she stammered.

"There was more what?" he asked. He wanted to help her, he just didn't know what she needed help with.

Samara opened her mouth, but before she could say anything his phone buzzed. It was still downstairs on the table, and although he didn't want anything to interrupt whatever Samara needed to get off her chest, it could be something about the stalker.

"I'll be right back," he told her, running back downstairs. In the kitchen, he snatched up his phone and saw a text from an unknown number.

Even before he opened it, he knew.

On the screen was a picture of a middle-aged woman sitting in the window of what looked like a café.

The accompanying caption read, 'Deliver Samara to me within the next hour or she dies'.

An hour.

Was that enough time for Tom and Chloe to find where this woman was and catch the stalker before he could kill her?

"Mike? What is it?"

Michael tried to turn the phone before Samara could see what was on it, but she must have followed him down because she was already right behind him and by her sharp intake of air, he knew she had already seen it.

"Don't worry," he said quickly. "I'm going to send this to Chloe and Tom. They have an hour. That should be enough time for them to track down this café."

"Or I could just do what he said." Her tone and her face were frantic. "We could set a trap. You could wire me, follow me, find out where he wants to meet, and then grab him when he comes for me."

While that might work, they could never set all of that up in just sixty minutes. "I can't let you do that," he said honestly. "Have faith, Samara. He messed up sending us a photo of his intended victim. We can find this café. We can find her. We can find him."

"Michael," she whimpered helplessly.

He could imagine what it felt like to be in Samara's position. To know that an innocent woman was going to die just because someone wanted to emotionally blackmail her into giving up her life. He wanted to say something to take her fears and pain away. He wanted to promise her that this would be over today.

Since he couldn't do any of those things, he did the only thing he could. He wrapped an arm around her, pulled her close, and held her tightly.

~

10:10 A.M.

Maeve Franklin sipped her coffee and ran through the mental checklist of jobs she needed to get done between now and Christmas.

Finish the Christmas shopping.

Buy groceries for the Christmas day family lunch.

Put up the last of the decorations.

Prepare the house for visiting relatives.

Pick up her in-laws from the airport.

Start work on the mountain of laundry that had taken over her dining room table.

Wrap gifts.

Dust.

Vacuum.

Sweep.

Mop.

Roast the turkey.

Cook the vegetables.

Make desserts.

Bake gingerbread cookies for her youngest's Christmas party at school.

There were probably another half a dozen things she had forgotten about, but that list was long enough to make her want to stay here in her favorite café, sipping her favorite coffee forever, and throw responsibility to the wind. Sometimes being an adult sucked.

At least she had a couple of days where she had the daytime mostly to herself. Her kids had another day of school, so today and tomorrow she could at least try to get a handle on things. Which was why she would give herself another ten minutes to sit and relax before she got to work on her mountain of a to-do list.

Reaching into her bag, Maeve pulled out her Kindle and opened her favorite book, two chapters, and then she'd leave.

The next few minutes flew by as she immersed herself in the imaginary land of books, and by the time she finished the second chapter she glanced up, surprised to see that nearly thirty minutes had passed. Reluctantly, she put her Kindle away and finished the last mouthful of coffee, then it was time to brace for the cold outside. She hated winter and was already counting down the days until summer would be back.

She put on her coat, her scarf, gloves, and a beanie and then picked up her bag and sighed miserably before heading outside. It wasn't that she didn't like Christmastime, she did, it was just that it was usually so busy that the whole day flew by, and she hadn't even had time to sit down and enjoy it.

But her kids enjoyed it, and that was enough for her. The smiles on their faces, their delight as they opened gifts, the fun they had playing with their cousins, overeating way too much junk food. That was what Christmas was all about, sharing the joy with the people you loved. She guessed she could put up with the snow and the cold for that.

And the snow was pretty.

Kind of.

She supposed.

At least like this when it was all fresh and white and covering everything in a dusting of powder. The trees lining the shopping strip were all strung with lights, and even though it wasn't even lunchtime yet it was dull, and the twinkling lights made everything look so merry.

Maeve wondered how many Christmases like this there would be. Her parents were getting older, her father's health hadn't been so good this year. And her in-laws were getting older as well, both of them were still healthy, but that couldn't last forever.

Her kids were getting older too. Her youngest had started fifth grade in the fall, next year he would be in middle school. Her middle one was thirteen now and was already embracing everything that being a teenager meant, Maeve was already preparing to battle a myriad of dramas with her daughter. And her oldest was sixteen, driving, had a part-time job. Next year he would be starting his final year of school then he would be out of the house and off to college. Would he still want to come home for Christmas, or would he want to go and spend it with a girlfriend's family? What about when her kids were grown and had families of their own, would there still be a Christmas gathering with all of them?

She missed the days when her kids were still small, and they had been so excited to leave out milk and cookies for Santa and carrots for the reindeer. She remembered how they would ask to go out into the yard after dark to see if they could see Rudolph's shiny nose in the black night sky. She remembered when they used to write letters to Santa and leave them on the floor by the chimney and then get so excited to wake up in the morning and find them gone. Maybe one day she could do all of those things with her grandchildren.

Looking both ways before she crossed the street, Maeve hurried to her car, quickly threw the shopping bags into the trunk, and then jumped inside, eager to get out of the cold. Sure, the snow might be pretty to look at, and it wouldn't feel like Christmas without it, but she still couldn't wait for it to go away.

It wasn't until she had clicked her seatbelt in and put the key in the ignition that she realized she wasn't alone in the car.

A strangled scream was cut short when something cold was shoved against her neck.

"Drive," a harsh voice demanded.

"P-please," she whimpered. Just moments ago her biggest worries had been the snow and the long list of chores she had to work her way through. Now she might never get that list finished. She might never see her family again. She might never even step out of this car again.

"I said drive." The man pressed the knife into the skin on her throat just deep enough to draw a trickle of blood to emphasize his point.

She didn't know what to do.

If she did as he said, then she was practically handing herself over to be murdered. There were people outside, all she had to do was roll down her window and scream for help. Could he slit her throat before someone came? Maybe if he realized she wasn't going to do as he wanted, he would just jump out of her car and run.

"Drive," the man hissed again. He sounded manic, possessed, and Maeve knew without a doubt that if she didn't do as he said then he would kill her.

Her hands were shaking as she put them on the steering wheel and started to drive. "P-please," she whispered again. "I have a family. I'll drive you wherever you want me to go, but please don't hurt me."

The man said nothing.

He just leaned up against the back of her seat and kept his knife at her neck.

What did he want from her?

Who was he?

Had he robbed a bank or something and wanted her to drive him away from the scene?

Was he a rapist?

A murderer?

"Wh-where do you want me to go?" she asked as she stopped at the end of the street.

"Turn left," he said like he didn't really care where they went.

If he didn't care where they went then why did he want her to drive him somewhere?

"Now right," he ordered.

She did as she was told.

"Pull over just up there."

They had only driven a block or so, and he wanted her to stop already?

"Please," she said again.

"Stop saying that," the man snapped.

Slowly, she lifted her gaze to the rear vision mirror. In it she saw the face of a man with short cut brown hair, big brown eyes, scarred skin, and a deformed ear. Was it also the face of her killer?

"I did what you asked. Let me go, please," Maeve begged.

"I told you to stop talking." The man moved the knife away from her neck and pressed his hands to his ears like he was trying to shut out more than just her voice. Maybe he was insane, and that was why he was doing this.

Since the knife was no longer at her throat, she had a chance to escape. All she had to do was undo her seatbelt, open her door, jump out, and run and not stop running until she got help.

"This will show them. This will teach them to keep what's mine away from me. This will make them give her back," the man was mumbling to himself. Maeve didn't know what he was talking about, and she didn't care. He was distracted, if she ran now, she didn't think he would even notice until it was too late, and she was already out of the car.

Her hand was on the door handle when the first blow came.

It got her right in the back, slicing in between her shoulder blades.

Pain flooded through her, and she cried out.

Another blow got her in the shoulder.

Maeve could feel her blood gushing out wetting her, it was warm and sticky and the more of it she lost, the colder she became.

She felt the third blow, and the fourth, by the fifth she was starting to fade.

After the eighth, she was gone.

~

10:39 A.M.

"Stop," Tom said.

Chloe immediately stopped the car. "What?"

"There." He pointed out the window at a café they had just passed. He held up the photo he'd been clutching as they drove around trying to find the location in the message Michael Stein had received. They only had twenty minutes left to find the woman in the photo before the stalker killed her. "Does that look like the café in the picture?"

His partner leaned over so she could get a clearer look. "I guess it kind of does."

She didn't sound convinced. "See there," he pointed to a corner of the picture where they could see the window frame, "that large dint, it looks like a car backed into it or something. And see there," Tom pointed at the corner of the window in the café they were parked in front of, "there's a dint there too, and it's in the right spot. And there, see the table in the window, in the picture you can just see that the chairs aren't all the same color. One is green, one is blue, and one is red. This café has the same arrangement of chairs."

"You notice everything," Chloe muttered under her breath.

His partner was right, he noticed everything, even the smallest of details. It was definitely an asset in his job as an FBI agent, although he wasn't as good at using the skill in his personal life. He'd missed major signals when he and Hannah had been married the first time, and it had led to them getting divorced. He was just lucky he had been given a second chance, and this time, he wasn't going to blow it. Now he had even more to lose. He and Hannah had a two-year-old daughter Noelle, and Hannah was four months pregnant with their second child. His family was his life, and he would never again let anything ruin his relationships with the people that were the most precious to him.

"Okay, you're right, I think this is the same café, but I don't see her. Anywhere," Chloe said, looking up and down the busy street.

"I don't either, but she might not have been gone long. Let's go in, take the photo, see if any of the staff recognize her. If we're lucky, she might be a regular, they might even know her name, and if we're really lucky, her car." Last time the stalker had followed his victims to their car and then struck in the relative safety of the parking garage. This was a different strip mall, but there was a parking garage down one end. If they were lucky, he would follow the same MO as last time.

They both climbed out of the car into the snowy morning. It was freezing, and Tom pulled his coat tighter around him while Chloe wrapped a scarf around her neck and shoved her hands into a pair of mittens. He couldn't help but roll his eyes when he saw that they had a Christmas scene embroidered on the backs of them. Chloe and her crazy Christmas clothes, usually she didn't wear them to work, but they were only three days away from Christmas, and she probably hadn't been able to resist.

It was a relief to step in out of the swirling snowflakes and wind and into the warmth and quiet of the café. It was busy, there was only one empty table, the one where the woman they were looking for had been sitting. Hopefully, that was a good thing and it meant that she had only just left.

"Excuse me," Tom said as he approached the counter. "I'm Special Agent Drake, and this is my partner, Special Agent Patrick. We're looking for this woman. Have you seen her?" He held out the photo so she could see it clearly.

"Did she do something wrong?" the young woman who looked no older than late teens asked, barely glancing at the photo.

He didn't have time to explain the entire situation, so he held the picture closer and said, "No, we believe she might be in danger. Have you seen her?"

The woman took the photo and gave it one quick look before she nodded. "I know her, she comes in all the time, pretty much every day."

Tom exchanged a quick glance with his partner, that was exactly what they wanted to hear. When Michael had called them to tell them about the message, they'd had copies of the picture made and sent to dozens of patrol cars that were sent to comb all the shopping malls in the area.

"Do you happen to know her name?" Chloe asked.

"I don't," the woman shook her head but then pointed to one of her colleagues, "but I think Missy might. Hey, Miss," she called to a slightly older woman who looked in her mid-twenties.

"Yeah?" The woman set a tray full of dirty cups down on the counter and came to join them.

"What's her name?" the girl asked as she passed the picture over. "She comes in all the time, and I've seen you talk to her."

"Her name is Maeve. Maeve Franklin. Who are you?" Missy asked them.

"Special Agent Drake and Special Agent Patrick," Tom replied.

"Like FBI Agents?" When they nodded, Missy asked, "Is Maeve in some sort of trouble?"

"We think that she might be in danger. She was in here earlier. Do you remember when she left?" Chloe asked.

Missy glanced at the clock on the wall. "Maybe, ten minutes ago."

"Do you remember anyone watching her? Anyone who left when she did? Anyone hanging around outside the café who seemed out of place?" Tom asked.

Both young women exchanged glances. "I didn't notice anything," the first woman said.

"Me either. As you can see, we're pretty busy, just keeping up with the orders is hard enough let alone paying attention to anything else," Missy added.

It was a long shot, but he had to ask. "You wouldn't happen to know what kind of car she drives, would you? Or where she might have parked it?"

"Actually, I do." The teenager nodded, her brown eyes sparkling with excitement. "Just a couple of days ago she left her phone behind on the table. I looked out the window and saw her getting into a car parked just across the street. I ran her phone out to her. She drives an SUV, it's green, bright green, it has a logo of the florist she works for on the side."

"Does she usually park in the street or in the parking garage down the end of the strip mall?" Chloe asked.

"The street," Missy said. "I often see the SUV out there. I didn't know it was Maeve's, but I see it all the time."

That was even better than he could ever have asked for.

"Thank you," Tom said, already turning to head back outside. They only had ten minutes left to find Maeve Franklin alive before the stalker followed through on his threat to kill her.

"We need to put out an APB on a green SUV with a florist logo on the side," Chloe said as they hurried back to the car.

"We should drive around for a bit, see if we can find them," Tom said as Chloe started the engine. "I know it's a long shot, but we've been lucky so far, who knows, we could find them. He's not going to try to hide the body because he wants us to find it. He wants us to know what the consequences are of disobeying him."

"Worth a shot," Chloe agreed as she pulled out into the busy Christmas traffic.

He called in what they knew about their victim and her vehicle and then turned his attention to searching the busy streets.

"Tom."

"What?" He turned from staring out the window to look at his partner.

"A green SUV," she said, pulling the car to a stop behind the other vehicle.

They approached cautiously, aware of how dangerous the stalker was. He didn't care who he had to hurt so long as he could do whatever it took to get to Samara.

He nodded at Chloe, and as she covered him, he opened the driver's door of the car.

Where he found Maeve Franklin lying slumped across the seats.

Tom already knew, but blind hope had him reaching out to touch his fingertips to the woman's neck.

He was right.

There was no pulse.

Maeve was already dead.

Stabbed dozens of times, just like the elderly woman in the parking garage.

Her body was still warm. The killer had only been gone a couple of minutes.

Just minutes earlier and they could have saved Maeve Franklin's life.

Minutes.

He knew better than most that life could change in just one minute.

That was all it took for things to be over.

～

12:36 P.M.

Samara pushed a piece of lettuce around on her plate. She didn't want to eat, but she didn't want to not eat because she knew that Michael was watching her like a hawk.

Another innocent person was dead because of her.

How could you eat after learning that?

Chloe and Tom had been too late to save her stalker's second victim. Well, third victim actually, since he had killed two people the first time.

Three lives ended all because someone wanted her.

Three people who wouldn't get to celebrate the holidays with their families.

Three people who wouldn't see in the new year in just over a week.

She felt numb.

There were too many emotions jumping around inside her that she couldn't feel any of them. It was the same thing that had happened after she found out about the first murders. It was her usual MO, when she got overwhelmed, her emotions just shut down, and she didn't feel them.

It was the only way she knew how to survive.

If she let her emotions become too strong, then she was afraid she would end up doing what she had tried and been unsuccessful at when she was thirteen.

Despite what Michael had said, it hadn't been just a cry for help. She *had* wanted to die. And for a long time afterward, she had been so upset that she had survived.

She had left school early one day, Fin was supposed to go to football practice after his final class, and her grandmother had bingo. She had gone through the medicine cabinet, taken whatever was there with a glass of water then gone to lie down in her bed to wait to die.

Only she hadn't died.

She had passed out. She remembered her eyes growing heavy and feeling sleepy, so very sleepy.

Then the next thing she knew, she was waking up in the hospital.

Apparently, Fin had skipped football practice because he had a party he wanted to go to that night and had come home to find her passed out. He'd called an ambulance, and she had been rushed to the hospital where her stomach had been pumped.

Her brother had been so angry with her, he thought that she had tried to abandon him like everyone else in their lives had, and he wasn't wrong. She'd been sent to a psychiatric facility where her therapist had taught her bonsai as a way to find the peace and tranquility she needed to learn to deal with the mess of emotions that lived inside her.

Even fifteen years later it was still her go-to.

But today she couldn't even summon the strength to do that.

She might not have suicidal thoughts anymore, but that didn't mean she always knew how to deal with her emotions. Often they overwhelmed her which she guessed was why her body had developed the defense mechanism of turning her numb.

"You've hardly eaten anything," Michael said, startling her out of her thoughts.

"Could you eat if you'd just gotten someone horribly murdered?" she asked dully.

"You didn't get anyone killed."

"Really? Because that's not what he said. He said that unless I gave myself up to him, he would kill someone, and that's exactly what he did."

"You are not responsible for his actions," Michael said fiercely, his brown eyes practically glowing with pent-up frustration. She knew it wasn't directed at her, it was directed at the stalker. Samara knew that he was angry because as well as killing innocent people the stalker was hurting her.

She didn't want to keep having this conversation, it was just going to continue going around in circles. She would keep saying that the stalker was killing because of her, and Michael would say that she wasn't responsible for someone else's actions, neither of them was going to change their positions.

Absently, she stuck her fork in the piece of lettuce she had been playing with and lifted it to her mouth. Samara knew that Chloe and Tom were working as hard as they could to catch the stalker and they very nearly had. Today's victim had been killed only minutes before they managed to find her car.

So close.

They had been so close to saving that woman's life and catching the stalker before anyone else got hurt. They had found the café, they had found out who the woman in the photo was, they had found out what car she drove, they had even managed to find the car.

And yet none of that had done any good.

She had been murdered anyway.

This was hopeless.

The stalker knew everything about her, and she knew nothing about him. He was going to keep picking random people off the street and killing them, and there was nothing they could do about it. How did you stop someone like that? How could you get ahead of them when there were too many potential victims out there?

This was hopeless.

The only way to stop him was to give him what he wanted.

Her.

If she gave herself over to him, then no one else had to die at his hands.

What other choice was there?

None.

There were no other choices, that was the reality of the situation.

They had tried using her as bait to catch him, and it hadn't worked. They had tried looking for him, and it hadn't worked. They had tried saving his victims before he could get to them, and it hadn't work. The only thing that was going to work was her doing what he asked.

Samara wanted to do it. Anything to stop the murders. The problem was, she didn't know how she was going to accomplish it.

She wasn't worried about how she would find the stalker, she had no doubt he was finding a way to keep watch on her house and would come to her the second she was on her own. The problem was, how was she going to get out of the house and be on her own? Not only was there always someone outside watching her house so the stalker didn't get to her, but Michael watched her like a hawk. It was like he knew what she wanted to do and was ready to tie her to her bed if necessary to stop her from doing it.

Upstairs earlier, he'd said such nice things about her, and she'd thought that maybe he'd been going to tell her he liked her as more than friends.

Never before had she considered the idea of her and Michael as a couple ... well, maybe she had. He'd starred in more than one of her fantasies, and they had so much fun together. Maybe she'd always hoped for more but not been willing to admit it.

Fear was holding Michael back, her too. She was just as afraid of taking the plunge from friendship to something more. She had tried to end her own life, and ever since, she had been trying to make up for it. Her suicide attempt had hurt the one person who had always been there for her, and she couldn't help but try to make up for that whatever the cost to herself. And trying so hard never to make another mistake was a heavy burden to bear.

"Here, I'll take your plate," Michael said, and Samara was surprised to see that she had finished the salad. Maybe she had been a little hungry after all.

"Thanks."

"What do you want to do this afternoon? Do you want to do your Christmas wrapping? Then we could put on a Christmas movie, light the fire, drink hot chocolate, and just chill out tonight."

She knew he was trying so hard to keep her mind off things, and she felt bad that she wasn't trying hard enough to work with him. She did have to wrap the gifts. After they got the message from her stalker, they'd called Chloe and Tom, then waited by the phone for news. When the agents had turned up on her doorstep, she had known without them having to say anything that they had been too late to save the stalker's next victim.

As much as Samara wasn't in the mood to look at garishly bright Christmas boxes and wrapping paper, or watch Christmas movies, she knew she had to meet Michael halfway, especially if she wanted to look for an opportunity to sneak out later.

Summoning a smile, she nodded. "Yeah, okay, we can do that."

"Great." Michael smiled back, looking relieved to know that she was still holding it together. He probably thought that meant she wouldn't do anything stupid like offer herself as a sacrifice. He was wrong, but he didn't need to know that, not until she was already long gone.

"I'll go get the gifts, they're still upstairs," she said, pushing back from the table.

"I'll clear the table and grab scissors and tape, then we can work in —" Michael broke off as the doorbell rang.

Panic immediately sliced through her, cutting away the numbness.

Was that Chloe and Tom again?

Surely the stalker hadn't killed again so soon, had he?

She couldn't take any more of this.

1:02 P.M.

"Relax, Samara, it's only Sawyer," Michael soothed when he saw panic flash across Samara's face. "It's not Tom and Chloe. No one else is dead. It's okay."

"Just Sawyer?" she repeated, still white as a ghost, still trembling, her eyes still full of barely controlled terror.

"Just Sawyer," he echoed.

He was worried about her.

She was hanging on by a thread, and he was terrified that at any second that thread could snap, and she would give herself over to her stalker so no one else died.

It was stressful situations like this that made him want to turn straight back to the bottle to dim the fear that swam inside him.

If Chloe and Tom didn't find the stalker soon, then Samara *would* sacrifice herself.

It was because she thought she had nothing to live for, no one to live for, and that her life was not as important as the lives of the people her stalker had and would kill. Michael knew it had to do with her suicide attempt as a teenager, and although he had thought the attempt was because of abandonment issues, it seemed from what Samara had said earlier that there was more to it than that.

He was afraid he knew what.

Young girl, acting out, then suddenly tries to kill herself. It didn't take a genius to figure out what was probably the cause.

Michael knew that both Samara and Fin had started getting into trouble at school when they went to live with their grandparents. He'd thought it was because of both their parents walking out on them, and for Fin that was probably the cause, but for Samara, it obviously ran a lot deeper than that.

"Come here," he said, wrapping his arms around her and drawing her close, holding her tight against his chest. "You're shaking," he murmured, holding her with one arm, and with his other he rubbed her back in small circles, hoping to calm her.

"What if it's not Sawyer?" she asked, her voice muffled against his chest.

"It is. He texted to say he was coming over." Michael pulled his phone from his pocket and pressed in the code, opening his messages and drawing Samara gently back so she could see the phone. "See?"

"Okay," she said, giving a shaky nod, then resolutely straightening her spine.

"Don't do that," he said, keeping hold of her when she would have darted out of his grip. "No one thinks you have to be perfect all the time, Samara."

"Sawyer's waiting," she said, her blue eyes refusing to meet his.

"Then he can just keep waiting. You are a beautiful, sweet, caring, kind, compassionate woman. You don't have anything in your past that you need to make up for. You did what you did, you had your reasons, I'm glad you weren't successful, but you don't have to try to be perfect because you did one thing that you regret."

Samara arched a brow at him like she didn't believe him.

He wished he knew what to say to convince her. When Sawyer was gone, they were going to have to have a talk because there was no way in hell he was allowing her to sacrifice herself because of misguided guilt.

"Come on." He caught her hand and pulled her with him through the foyer to the front door.

"Everything okay?" Sawyer asked when he opened the door, giving both him and Samara an assessing once over.

"Fine," Samara replied quickly.

"Come on in," Michael said and closed the door behind his friend when he stepped into the foyer.

"Savannah sent a whole box of goodies," Sawyer said, holding out a white box. His friend's twin sister loved to bake around the holidays and always made much more than she and her husband could eat and was always sharing stuff around.

"I thought she might not have time this year to do her usual baking, now that she has Mason." He well remembered how hard it had been to get things done with a toddler always underfoot.

"My nephew might be only four months old, but Savannah made sure he knows not baking at Christmas is not an option." Sawyer laughed.

"Is she still making her gingerbread Christmas creation on Christmas Eve?" he asked. It was another one of Savannah's traditions and one that never ceased to amaze him. If she ever decided she had had enough of her job working at the FBI's evidence recovery team, then she could open up her own bakery.

"Since Christmas Eve is also Asher's birthday, she's making a train. You know how obsessed Asher is with them."

"That's cute." Michael cast a glance at Samara who was standing beside him, her hand still clamped in his, staring listlessly at the floor.

"We were going to wrap Christmas gifts if you want to help," he said to Sawyer.

"Sure, sounds like fun," Sawyer agreed. "Ashley won't let me wrap any of ours other than mine for her because she thinks I don't fold the paper at the corners properly, but I enjoy wrapping gifts."

"Actually, I think I might go lie down for a while, I have a headache," Samara said.

She looked like she wasn't feeling well, but Michael didn't know if she wanted to lie down because she wasn't feeling well or if she just wanted some time alone so she could figure out a way to sneak out of here. "Do you need some painkillers?" he asked, wanting to give her the benefit of the doubt.

"No, I think it's just stress, I just need to close my eyes for a bit and I'm sure it will go away."

"All right, we're down here if you need anything."

Samara pulled her hand, and he reluctantly let it go, slowly, letting their fingers touch for as long as possible. Then he watched her drag herself up the stairs. He really wished he knew what to say to help her. That same thought kept running through his head, but he couldn't come up with an answer.

"H-hmm."

"I don't have a good feeling about this," he said, still staring at the top of the stairs where Samara had disappeared down the hall.

"I know," Sawyer said. And he really did. He had gone through almost this exact same thing only twelve months ago when a serial killer had been determined to kill Ashley.

"This is such a mess," he muttered helplessly.

He wanted a drink.

Badly.

It was all he could do not to jump in his car and go and buy a six-pack and drink them all in one go.

If there was any alcohol in the house, he probably would have succumbed to temptation already.

"You know what you have to do, right?" Sawyer asked. "If you don't want her to give in to the pressure the stalker is putting on her."

"I have to tell her how I feel about her. I just don't know if I can."

"You have to. She needs to hear it. I get the fear of taking a friendship and putting it on the line to see if there's more there, but it worked out for me and Ashley."

"That was different," he protested immediately.

"How? Ashley and I were best friends. I knew she didn't feel the same way as I did, but with everything that was going on it all came out, and I'm glad it did. If it hadn't, we wouldn't be getting married in three days. That could be you and Samara this time next year. You want that, I know you do."

"Every time I think about saying the words, I can't get them out," he admitted. Fear was a powerful thing, as was guilt, and both could easily rule your life.

"Because of Heidi?"

"Yeah."

"I get guilt, especially over someone's death. After my dad's death, I felt guilty. I wasn't even there when it happened, but I kept thinking that if I was then maybe things would have turned out differently. What happened, happened. I wish it hadn't, I'd do anything to have him still alive, and I wish that your daughter was still with you. If she was, what would she want you to do?"

That was easy.

Heidi was like a little ball of sunshine all wrapped up in a tiny little package. She had a wild mess of brown curls and the biggest green eyes that shimmered with joy and excitement. She laughed all the time and very rarely cried. She loved to sing and dance, she always had music playing, even when she was sleeping. She loved cuddles and kisses and would climb out of her crib during the night and come and climb into his bed to snuggle. She was his beautiful, happy, loving little princess.

She was his heart.

And she wouldn't want him to give up a chance to be with the other person who shared his heart.

"She'd want me to be happy."

"Does Samara make you happy?"

She did.

She was the only person since his daughter's death that gave him a sense of peace, that quietened the screaming guilt inside him.

In many ways they were very similar, which allowed him to relax and not constantly fight himself when he was with her.

"She does," he said softly.

"Then you know what you have to do."

4:18 P.M.

She looked terrible.

Samara stood at the vanity in her bathroom and stared at her reflection. Her color was bad, the bruises from when she had jumped out of the stalker's car were starting to change color, a little less black and blue, and a little more yellow and green. Her head still drummed a steady beat of pain that had been there ever since her near abduction. Headache aside, she wasn't really feeling any other effects from the concussion. All she felt was a growing sense of desperation to do whatever it took to put an end to her stalker's reign of terror.

No one else was going to die for her.

She had nothing to lose by giving herself.

Yes, she had her brother and his family, and yes, she had friends she loved, and yes, she enjoyed her job, but realistically she didn't have as much to lose as the people the stalker might kill next.

Or those he already had.

When she had left Michael and Sawyer downstairs, she had laid down for a few minutes. She hadn't been lying about the headache, and she had intended to take a power nap so that her head was clear and able to figure out a way out of her house without getting caught. But the second she had closed her eyes, she'd known sleep was never going to come. Her head was too full of jumbled thoughts and emotions.

So instead of sleep, she had pulled out her laptop and put her computer skills to use finding out whatever she could about the people who had died in her place.

The first victims were Brighton and Christine Morginson. Both were seventy-six, they had been married for over fifty years. Brighton had been a mechanic before retiring shortly after his sixtieth birthday, and Christine had taught Sunday School at her church and still assisted the current teacher. They had three children, ten grandchildren, and four great-grandchildren.

The woman who had died today was forty-six-year-old Maeve Franklin. Mother of three, a ten-year-old son, a thirteen-year-old daughter, and another son who was sixteen. She managed a chain of florists across the city and had an ailing father who she spent a lot of time taking care of.

They were all good people who hadn't done anything wrong. They hadn't deserved what had happened to them, and there was no way she could stand by and let it happen to anyone else.

So, she was out of here.

Hopefully, Sawyer was still here, and Michael was busy talking with his friend. If they were in the living room, they would see her as she came down the stairs if they had left the door open. If they were in the sunroom, then it would make it harder to get out the backdoor since it was in there. But there was a third exterior door from the garage. If she could get to that then she was home free.

The Hawthorns who lived in the house behind hers were away on vacation visiting his family. Samara knew because she was reasonably friendly with her neighbors, and they had asked her to bring in their mail for them. Once she was in her backyard, she could jump the fence into theirs and then walk around to the front and onto the other street and whoever's turn it was to watch her house would never be any the wiser that she was gone.

Before she could overthink things, Samara switched off the bathroom light and tiptoed quietly to the top of the stairs. She couldn't hear anything so she walked down, trying to look as casual as she could in case she was noticed. The living room was empty, so she crept closer to the sunroom to try to hear if Michael and Sawyer were in there. Again, it appeared the room was empty, maybe Michael was outside saying goodbye to Sawyer, or maybe Sawyer had already left, and Michael was in the bathroom, or taking a nap, or something.

Whatever the case, it looked like a sign she was doing the right thing.

Without hesitating since Michael could come back at any second, she hurried through the sunroom and out into the backyard. She went straight to the fence, dragging over a potted plant so she could use the large terracotta pot as a steppingstone to get up and over the face.

Samara had just hoisted herself up onto the fence and was about to swing a leg over when an arm wrapped around her waist, and she was lifted down and set on the grass.

"Just let me go, Mike," she begged.

"You know I can't do that."

"This is best for everyone." Michael still had a hold of her, and she sagged in his grip.

"It's not best for me," Michael countered.

"You have other friends. People are *dying*."

"So, what? You're going to go and die instead?" he asked harshly.

She just shrugged.

It was an easy choice.

People with families who had nothing to do with this whole mess dying, or her dying?

What other choice was there to make?

Michael grabbed her by the shoulders and spun her around. His dark brown eyes were a tumultuous mess of emotions, and she could read on his face what he was going to say even before he said it.

"You can't die," he said softly. "I can't lose you as well. I love you, Samara." He dipped his head and brushed his lips across hers.

Then he shoved her up against the fence, his hands spanning her waist, holding her in place, his body right up against hers, and his mouth crushed against hers. Her lungs should scream for air, for her to take a breath, but they didn't because they didn't need to. Michael was giving her what she needed—needed more than oxygen.

As soon as their lips touched, she felt it.

A jolt of electricity.

Something passed between them.

All those fears about whether or not their friendship could turn into something more or if they'd ruin what they already shared melted away with his mouth on hers.

This felt right.

Better than right.

It felt perfect.

It felt like she belonged somewhere for the first time, with someone who really and truly wanted her.

"Still want to leave? Still think you have nothing to live for and no one who would care if you weren't here?" he murmured against her lips.

"No," she whispered, a little breathily. She still wanted this to end, and she still didn't want anyone else to have to die for her, but she didn't want to hurt Michael by offering herself up to her stalker.

"Good." She felt him relax like he had hoped what he'd done had been enough to sway her and get her to stay.

She tensed. "Is that why you kissed me? So I wouldn't leave and go to the stalker?"

"Do you really think I would do that? You felt what I did when we kissed, I know you did. You know that was real. I've liked you for a long time, but I didn't think I deserved to be happy after what I did to Heidi. But you and I are so alike, and although I fought against it, I couldn't stop my feelings for you from growing. I've only ever felt love this strong for one other person, and I killed her. I'm so afraid that loving you is somehow going to get you hurt as well."

"Michael," she whispered, his sorrow and pain just about crushing her. She lifted her hands and held his face between them, guiding it down so she could kiss him again. "Heidi's death was an accident, and nothing is going to happen to me. It's because you're here with me that the stalker hasn't come for me again. You being here has *saved* me."

They were both so messed up. Could two people like them really have a successful relationship even if they did love one another?

Could she risk starting a relationship knowing that he could hurt her and walk away just like everyone else in her life had?

Could she throw it all away and spend the rest of her life alone just because she was afraid?

She wanted to take this risk.

And it *was* a risk for her.

But not taking it meant that when she was seventy-six like Brighton and Christine Morginson, all she would see when she looked back at her life was regrets. She wanted to look back on her life and see all the amazing things she had done and all the amazing family who loved her.

"Let's go inside, upstairs," she said, pressing a kiss to his jaw, his stubble prickly against her lips.

"Upstairs?" he asked, cocking an eyebrow.

Laying her heart bare she said the words aloud, "I love you too, Mike."

~

4:42 P.M.

Did he hear her right?

Did Samara just say that she loved him too?

"You heard me," she said softly, pressing another kiss to his jaw.

"You do?" Michael still wasn't quite ready to believe it.

"I never thought about being anything other than friends until we talked in the hospital the day after the stalker tried to kidnap me. I never really considered the possibility of falling in love. I had deluded myself into thinking I was okay with spending the rest of my life alone. But I'm not. I don't want to be alone for the rest of my life, I've already spent the first half that way, and I don't want to miss out on a chance to have everything I ever wanted because I'm scared."

So, this was just about her not wanting to be alone?

Was he just someone to keep her company?

It was hard to believe that a woman would ever want to be with him after he had killed his own child.

"No one has ever made me feel safe like you do," Samara said. Her arms circled his waist, and she pressed her ear to his chest, right over his heart.

He ran his fingers through her thick dark hair. "These feelings might be new to you, but they're not to me. I've loved you for a long time now. You have a lot going on right now, maybe what you think you're feeling is just reflecting back what you see in me and not what's really in your heart." Hurting her was the last thing he wanted to do, but he had to be sure. He had to know that it wasn't her fear speaking but that these feelings she said she had come from a real place. Losing his daughter and battling his addiction were the hardest things he had ever had to do, and he didn't think he could go through either again. He couldn't lose Samara. If he did, he would turn straight back to the bottle, only this time, he didn't think he'd have the strength to beat the addiction that wanted to claim him.

Samara's grip on him tightened, and when she spoke, she didn't sound angry or hurt. "Don't be afraid, Michael. Please. I'm scared too. This is hard. For both of us. We're both messed up inside, it's what drew us together, we get each other, it's what makes us such good friends. I'm so scared of what the stalker will do, to me, to all those innocent people out there that he decides to go after. But I don't want to be scared of this, of what's between us. This could be the easiest thing in the world if we don't fight it, if we don't dwell on all the reasons why we think it won't work, or why we don't deserve to have it work. It's happening, Mike." She turned her face into his chest. "This is happening whether we like it or not. We're falling in love."

When she said it, it sounded so simple.

Lay everything else aside and just feel.

It was the problem for people like them who lived in their heads, who overthought and overanalyzed everything. It was hard sometimes to just let go and go with what you felt.

But Sawyer was right. Heidi would want him to go after what made him happy.

And Samara was right, this was happening. They shouldn't fight it.

Michael scooped her up into his arms, cradling her like she was the most precious thing in the world because she was.

Without letting his brain talk him out of it, he let his lips do what came naturally: to find Samara's and kiss her like she was the only thing that existed.

Just the two of them.

She'd asked him to take her upstairs, so that was what he was going to do.

He didn't stop kissing her as he carried her inside and up the stairs. Heading straight for Samara's bedroom, he laid her out on the bed, then took a moment just to look at her. Bruises aside, she was stunning. He loved her eyes, they were a gorgeous shade of summer sky blue, but it wasn't the color that he loved, it was what was inside them. It was the haunted gleam that she tried to hide but that he saw as clearly as he saw that her eyes were blue. It was what had drawn him to her the first day they had met. He had known from that moment that he wanted to do whatever it took to one day wipe it away. He wanted her to be happy, he wanted her to be able to let go of the past so she could have a future, and he loved that she wanted the same thing for him.

"Is something wrong?" Samara asked uncertainly.

"No, not wrong, perfect, everything is perfect."

"Then why are you just staring at me?"

"Because I want to savor every second of this. Every second of *you*." Almost reverently, he reached out and traced his fingertips down her cheek. Her skin was so soft, he wanted to devour every single inch of it with his fingers and his tongue.

"The more you stare at me like that, the more I want you," Samara said breathily.

He laughed, and the last of the tension and fear that had been inside him vanished. This was what he wanted, Samara was what he wanted, and he could have her. The only thing standing between him and happiness was himself. Did he really want to let this slip through his fingers?

No.

He didn't.

He might still think he was responsible for Heidi's death, but this wasn't just about him. Samara needed him, even better, she wanted him. If he threw this away then he would be hurting her.

That was something he couldn't do.

He unzipped her hoodie, revealing a simple white bra and a flat stomach that he couldn't help but touch. They worked out together in the gym most nights after work, so it wasn't like he hadn't seen her stomach before, but somehow he'd never seen her like this. It was like seeing her in a whole new light.

"You're stunning," he said, more to himself than to Samara. Her pale skin with her dark hair and bright blue eyes was a gorgeous combination, and he could hardly believe that someone this beautiful was letting him touch her, and kiss her, and make love to her.

"You're pretty stunning yourself, or you would be if you would hurry up," she said wryly, moving restlessly beneath him.

Michael laughed again and climbed onto the bed kneeling over her. "I never knew you were so impatient."

"Only when it's something I really want," she said, reaching up to undo his pants.

"Uh, uh, uh," he caught her hands in one of his and pulled them up, pinning them above her head. "No rushing. We can do it your way next time, but this time we're taking our time." To prove his point, he kissed her impossibly lightly and then trailed a line of equally light kisses down her neck, between her breasts, and down her stomach stopping just above her pants.

"Mike," she groaned, squirming.

He wanted to give her what she wanted, and he wanted to torment her a little longer because this was something he had dreamed about for a long time now and he wanted it to never end.

In the end, his impatient Samara made the decision for him by pushing up on her elbows and shoving his pants down his thighs, and reaching into his boxers, claiming his hard length with her nimble fingers and making him groan. No way was he coming this quickly like an inexperienced adolescent.

"Okay, okay," he said, grabbing her hand and uncurling her fingers one by one. "You got what you wanted." He climbed off the bed, shed his jeans and boxers, pulled a condom from his pocket, and slid it on, then pulled off Samara's sweatpants and panties and tossed them on the floor.

Then he was between her legs, slipping a finger inside her to stretch her and prepare her to take him. She was wet, and he groaned again liking the idea that he turned her on, made her body weep for his touch.

"Hurry up, Mike," she said, her hips thrusting restlessly. "You're going to make me come, and I don't want to until you're inside me."

Swirling his thumb across her little bundle of nerves, he withdrew his fingers and slid into her in one smooth thrust. His mouth claimed hers again, and he kissed her as his hands roamed her body, wanting to feel every single inch of her, wanting their bodies to be joined forever. They moved as one, and it didn't take long for that feeling to take hold deep in his belly, growing and working its way out until it consumed him.

Samara murmured his name as she tumbled over the edge, and a second later he joined her, falling into an ocean of bliss as wave after wave of ecstasy washed over him. Balancing his weight so he didn't crush her, Michael laid on top of her for a moment longer, not quite ready to leave the warmth of Samara's body.

This was where he wanted to be.

This was the only place he wanted to be.

It was even better than he had dreamed about.

Throwing away something this beautiful, this perfect, that made him feel this good would be a mistake.

For the first time in his life, he was in love, and he wasn't going to let anyone ruin it. Not Samara and her fears, not the stalker and his obsession, and not himself and his guilt.

~

9:20 P.M.

Samara yawned and opened her eyes.

"Hey, sleepyhead."

She lifted her head to see Michael looking down at her. They were still in her bed although it looked like only she had been sleeping, Michael was sitting beside her, propped up against the headboard, his laptop in his lap. She didn't even remember falling asleep, one moment she had been snuggled in Michael's arms after they made love, and now she was waking up.

"How long was I asleep?" she asked, fighting another yawn.

"Couple of hours."

"Sorry." She rubbed at her eyes and sat up. Falling asleep right after sex wasn't the best impression, especially when it was the first time they'd had sex.

"Don't be sorry, you needed the rest. You're recovering from a concussion, and after everything that's gone on the last few months with your stalker, plus the stress of the last few days, your body decided it had had enough."

He was right, she just wished that her body had held out a little longer. Lying in Michael's arms had almost been better than making love. She liked this. Waking up with someone there beside her instead of all alone was wonderful. It was something so simple, and yet it meant so much to her.

"What were you doing while I slept?" she asked, looking at the laptop screen. It looked like he was running a search.

"Just the usual, trying to figure out who this guy is and where you met him," Michael answered.

Thinking of her stalker pulled her out of the warm, fuzzy cocoon she had been in since Michael pulled her off the fence.

Back to reality.

The little break had been nice, but nothing had changed.

Well, one thing had changed, she and Michael were together now, but as far as the stalker went, he was still out there, and he was still going to keep killing people until he got what he wanted. As much as she hated knowing that more people would die because of her, she didn't think she could offer herself up to him now. If she threw her life away so that no one else got hurt, that would devastate Michael. He had already lost his daughter, which he blamed himself for, if he lost her too, he would blame himself because he was her bodyguard. In his mind, if she were hurt while he was responsible for her safety it would be his fault.

"Did you find anything?" Samara asked.

"No, I'm sorry. But we will find him."

That's what she had been telling herself for months now, but so far no one had been able to find him.

She was starting to lose hope they ever would.

He could keep killing people indefinitely.

And sooner or later, even if she didn't give herself up, he was going to make another play for her. He couldn't let it go. He wanted her, and he wasn't ever going to stop until he got her. Michael and the rest of her friends, and Chloe and Tom, and the cops would all do everything they could to try to keep her safe, but there were no guarantees in life, and the stalker might get her anyway.

"I promise you, Samara, I will *never* let him lay a hand on you. I won't let anyone else hurt you ever again," Michael said fiercely, slipping an arm around her shoulders.

She wanted to believe that.

So badly.

But if life had taught her anything it was that pain was waiting around every corner, and that sooner or later everyone walked out on you.

Not Michael though, she couldn't imagine him ever doing anything to hurt her or ever walking away from her. They were so similar, he knew how much that would devastate her. Putting herself out there and letting go of her fear for a chance at happiness was a big deal. It wasn't the same as it was for most people, most people risked their hearts for happiness every day, but when you had lost as much as she had as early on in her life as she had, then it became so much harder.

"Was it your dad or your grandfather?" Michael asked, breaking the silence.

"What?" she asked, confused by the sudden change in conversation.

"Who hurt you."

Samara felt the color drain from her face.

Her blood grew icy cold, and she shivered.

She had enough on her plate to deal with right now without dredging up the past.

"I'm a little hungry, I might go and make some dinner. Do you want anything?" she asked as she threw back the covers and climbed out of bed.

Michael caught her hand. "Don't walk away, Samara. I'm here because I care. I love you. You never told anyone, did you?"

"So, you don't want anything?" she said, trying desperately to pull her hand out of Michael's iron grip. Why was he pushing this when it was clear she didn't want to talk about it? Couldn't he leave well enough alone?

"It was your grandfather, wasn't it? You went to live with them when you were ten, he split two years later, and then just a year after that you tried to kill yourself."

"Michael," she pleaded, wishing he would just stop talking. They could have a late dinner, make love again, then go to sleep in each other's arms. *That* was what she wanted, not an interrogation about her messed-up childhood.

"I'm sorry." He finally released her hand and climbed out of bed, rounding it to stand in front of her. "I'm so sorry that happened to you."

A million denials ran through her head.

She wanted to scream at him for even suggesting it. She wanted to cry that nothing like that had ever happened to her. She wanted to go running out of here and make dinner and pretend like this conversation had never happened.

Instead, she just stood there like a statue.

She didn't move as Michael wrapped his arms around her and held her. He gently guided her back to sit on the bed, fluffing pillows up behind her and tucking the covers around her. He slid back into the bed beside her and took her freezing hands in his and rubbed them.

Slowly, his warmth began to seep into her and pulled her out of her daze.

"Don't tell my brother," she whispered desperately. "Fin doesn't know, and I don't ever want him to find out. He's already so angry with me for what I tried to do. He was the one who found me, he thought I wanted to leave him too. I don't want him to know what happened. Please, Mike, please. Don't tell him. Promise me. Mike, promise me you won't say anything," she begged. She was quickly switching from dazed to hysterical.

"Shh, sweetheart." Michael drew her against him. "If you don't want to tell him then I won't say anything, but I don't think he'll be angry. At least not with you. With your grandfather and what he did to you, but you didn't do anything wrong."

"I did," she contradicted, "I tried to kill myself."

"Because you were a little girl who was sexually abused for two years by someone who should have taken care of her. You didn't know how to process what had happened, and you didn't have anyone you could tell. You didn't do anything wrong, Samara. Reacting to trauma is not a crime, you did what you did, no judgment from me, you don't have to try to be perfect with me. When we're together you can drop the perfectionist thing and just be you. You can cry if you need to cry, you can get angry if you need to get angry, you can laugh if you want to laugh, you're safe with me, safe to just be you."

His words brought tears to her eyes, and it wasn't long before they were tumbling down her cheeks. She'd never cried like this in front of anyone before. Tears flooded freely down her face, and deep, chest heaving sobs wracked through her. Michael held her, stroking her hair and murmuring to her in a soothing voice until her tears were spent.

In a way, she was glad that he knew. If they were going to be a couple, then it would be nice not to keep this secret from him. Other than the therapist who had treated her in the psychiatric hospital after her suicide attempt, no one other than her and her grandfather knew what he had done to her. Holding onto that secret for so many years had been a heavy burden to carry, and knowing that Michael knew and didn't see her any differently was more of a relief than she could ever express.

Michael wiped away the last of her tears with his knuckles then pressed a kiss to her forehead. "Want to have some dinner now?"

She shook her head. She was tired, that kind of bone-deep weariness that took hold of your entire body and wouldn't let go. She didn't want to eat, she didn't want to talk, she didn't want to feel, she didn't want to think.

"Hold me," she said, snuggling closer.

Michael did. He wrapped his arms around her and shuffled them both down the bed so they were lying on their sides facing each other.

"Sleep now, sweetheart, I got you."

This was what she wanted.

This was what she needed.

Content, Samara closed her eyes and drifted off to sleep.

# CHAPTER

## *Four*

December 23rd
6:38 A.M.

Why wasn't it working?

Dante stomped around the cabin screaming at the top of his lungs.

This was all wrong.

All wrong.

He'd killed three people. They knew what he was capable of so why were they still keeping Samara from him?

He knew that they had found the bodies—for a fact. He'd only just killed the woman in the SUV and climbed into his own car further down the block when he'd seen those FBI agents show up. He had sat for a moment watching them open the car, find the body, see all the blood, knowing that they were responsible for that woman's death, before driving off and coming back here.

And he knew that they knew who had killed them. He had left a message in the blood of the old couple at the parking garage, and since he didn't know Samara's phone number—they kept making her change it—he had sent a photo of his next intended victim to the man charged with being Samara's bodyguard. The FBI Agents had been quick tracking him down. They had obviously managed to find the café and the woman's identity if they had known what her car looked like. They had very nearly caught him, but he didn't care, it was worth the risk. *Samara* was worth the risk.

So why wasn't it enough?

Why were they disobeying him?

Why were they willing to put the whole neighborhood at risk?

He stopped stomping around and dropped down onto the couch in front of the fireplace.

Dante had expected her to be here by now.

Everything was ready for her, everything was perfect. All that was missing was Samara.

He didn't know what he was going to do if this didn't work.

Obviously, picking random people off the street wasn't the answer. The people watching Samara, keeping her from coming to him, didn't seem to care about those he had already killed and those he would.

So maybe he had to change track.

If they didn't care about strangers, then maybe they would care if he went after one of them.

That could be the answer.

And it wasn't like he had anything to lose. If this didn't work, then he would simply find something that did.

Nothing was going to keep him from Samara.

Nothing.

He would fight for her with every fiber of his being. He would do whatever it took. They could throw him in prison, they could lock Samara in a safe house, they could move her to the ends of the earth, and he would find her. He would find a way for the two of them to be together.

Dante was confident with his new plan to go after one of the people who was keeping the woman he loved away from him, then they could see how it felt. The ache in your chest that no medicine could cure, the hole in the pit of your stomach, the feeling of half of your soul missing. See how they liked it.

There were plenty of options to choose from. He would have to put some thought into it to try to figure out what would make the biggest impact on those who stood between him and Samara.

As much as he thought this new plan would work where the last one had failed, what if it didn't?

What would he do next?

He felt panic grow inside him.

It welled up, and he lurched back to his feet and resumed stomping.

What would he do if he never got Samara?

He'd never stop trying but trying didn't always mean succeeding.

He would rather be dead than not have Samara.

He would rather she be dead than have to live without her.

Was that a possibility?

If this didn't work, maybe he could do something that would kill both him and Samara—and anyone trying to get in his way—and that way, they would be together for eternity.

That was an enticing idea. This world wasn't a good place, it was too full of pain and evil, but the afterlife was a place of peace and calm. He would miss not having her here, especially since he had gone to so much trouble to make this place just perfect, a home that would have been a happy one. And it could still work that way, but if it didn't, he might consider ending both their lives together so that they could be united in death.

Dante wanted to spend eternity with Samara, but he also wanted her here. He wanted to kiss her and touch her and make love to her, then they could travel into the next world.

This had to work.

It had to.

He stormed out of the house and into the cold, snowy night. He had to cleanse himself from his wicked and doubtful thoughts. He had to cleanse his body so that he could cleanse his mind and his soul.

Dante stripped of his shoes, his sweater, shirt, pants, socks, and underwear, dropping them at his feet, then he stood naked in the middle of the yard. Snowflakes danced about him, and the wind whipped through his short hair, goosebumps broke out all over his skin, but he relished the cold.

Cold was cleansing.

And right now, he needed to be cleansed.

It wasn't enough.

Standing here wasn't enough.

Dante threw himself down into the snow that was piled a foot high and began to grab handfuls of it, rubbing it over every inch of his body. He couldn't leave a single spot untouched. He scrubbed as hard as he could, raking his nails along with each rub so that the snow could almost get inside him.

When he was satisfied he had done a good job, Dante sunk into the snow, stretching out in it, enjoying the way his limbs tingled with the cold. He stared up at the sky. It was full of clouds and the snow coming down was pretty thick, but he could still see the faint glow where the moon was going down and the lightening of the sky where the sun would soon be rising.

A new day was coming.

Today was going to be the day.

The snow had rejuvenated him, freshened him and his resolve. He knew that what he had planned next would work, any thoughts that it wouldn't had been washed away. Of course he would be successful. Why would he not be?

It had been a long couple of days, and he had barely slept. He needed to get some rest, then he would be clear-headed to figure out exactly what he had to do.

Gathering his clothes, he headed back inside, pleased to see that his skin was ruddy and red from the snow. He liked that. Samara needed a little more color on her pale skin. Maybe when he brought her here, the two would play out in the snow until they were both red and invigorated.

Dropping his clothes and shoes by the front door, Dante didn't bother to put them on or to get clean ones from the closet, he had other things on his mind. Mainly sleep and then he'd get on his computer and figure out who he was going to target and how he would do it.

The fire still raged in the fireplace, the flames dancing about much as the snowflakes had outside. It was mesmerizing. He stretched out on the sofa on his side so he could watch as he went to sleep. As he lay there, he thought about Samara. Was she thinking about him? Was she hoping that he would hurry up and get to her? Was she trying to figure out a way to get out of her house and away from those who sought to destroy their love so she could come to him?

"Don't worry, my sweet Samara," Dante said aloud. "I'm coming for you. I'm *coming* for you. I'm going to bring you here to the home I chose for us. I'm going to give you the Christmas of your dreams, I'm going to spoil you like the beautiful, special princess that you are. I'm going to love you forever. I'm not ever going to let you go. Not ever. Not for anything. It's going to be just the two of us for all eternity. We're going to live together and then we're going to die together, and nothing and no one is going to come between us. You're mine, sweet Samara, you are mine to love and cherish, and that's what I'm going to do."

Fixing his gaze on the flames, Dante let his mind relax, just a couple of hours sleep and then he'd get to work. Today was going to be the first day of the rest of his life.

~

8:17 A.M.

"I hope you don't mind us coming over so early," Hannah Drake said when Samara and Michael opened the front door.

Hannah had her two-year-old daughter's hand held tightly in her left hand, and almost two-year-old Asher's hand held tightly in her right. Both toddlers were bouncing up and down with excitement, their cheeks pink from the cold, their eyes sparkling, big smiles on their little faces.

"Aunt Sami," Asher squealed, wriggling out of Hannah's grip to wrap himself around her legs. He couldn't say her name yet, so he always called her Sami, it reminded her of when she was a very small girl and Fin used to call her that.

"Hey, buddy," Samara said, picking up her nephew and getting a big wet kiss on the cheek. "Come on in," she said to Hannah, who led Noelle inside.

"We thought we'd come by for a visit since you're stuck in here," Hannah explained, removing her coat and her daughter's. "I was going to come later this morning, but when I told these two we were going to visit you, they were so excited they couldn't wait, so sorry we're here so early."

"That's okay, we were both up," Michael said.

After their talk last night, she had slept straight through to six o'clock. It had been good sleep too, restful and quiet, not haunted by bad dreams that had her constantly waking and tossing and turning. As though even in sleep his body was attuned to hers, Michael had woken only a minute or so after her and had persuaded her—fairly easily—to take a shower together.

Samara had never had sex in the shower before. What her grandfather had done to her at such a young age had altered how she saw sex. It wasn't something she had looked forward to doing like the other girls at school, and while she had done it a couple of times, it was never something she had enjoyed, just something she had done to prove to herself that she wasn't too scared.

But with Michael it was different.

With Michael, it had been everything she had wished it could be.

"We're happy to have you guys here," Samara said, smiling at Hannah and the toddlers.

Asher squirmed in her arms, so she set him down and watched as he and Noelle chased each other about.

She had never really thought about having kids before, not because she didn't like them or that she didn't want them, but because she had never foreseen that she would be in a relationship and so in a place to have a baby. But now ...

Now she wasn't really sure.

She and Michael hadn't discussed anything yet. Were they officially a couple? Were they dating? Were they going to live together once this was over? Were they going to get married one day? Were they going to have kids? All she knew was that they loved each other and had spent an amazing night together with mind-blowing sex and the best sleep she'd ever had.

But she wanted more than that.

Now that she'd had a taste of what it could be like to be in a relationship with someone she loved and share their lives rather than living a solitary life, she knew she wasn't willingly going to give it up.

Samara couldn't stop her gaze from moving to Hannah's stomach. Her friend was four months pregnant and just beginning to show. She wondered what it felt like to know that a person growing inside you was half you and half the person you loved.

"Okay, munchkins," Michael rounded up the kids, "who wants cookies and chocolate milk?"

"I do, I do," the toddlers jumped up and down.

"That okay?" Michael asked Hannah.

"Sure, I don't think sugar could get them any more excited than they already are."

"Call out if you need anything," Michael told her, leaning over to give her a quick kiss before taking the kids into the kitchen.

Samara felt her cheeks heat. She hadn't known that they were telling people that they were together, but apparently, they were. They really needed to sit down later and talk some things through so that they were on the same page.

"So, you guys are finally together?" Hannah asked with a smile when Michael, Noelle, and Asher disappeared through the door.

"I guess so." She smiled back.

"About time."

It seemed like everyone had known that she and Michael belonged together except her and Michael. "It's weird, it feels so right now, but I never really thought about there being anything other than friendship between us, not until all of this happened. I guess looking back I always knew it, but I just never acknowledged it. We both had a lot to lose taking that step from being friends to being a couple."

"You both also have a lot to gain."

That was true.

Now that they had laid their fears aside, they both had a chance to be happy. Really and truly happy.

There was just something Samara was still unsure about.

"Can I ask you something?" she asked Hannah.

"Sure." Hannah smiled, but from the look in her eyes, she knew it was going to be a question she wouldn't like.

"Let's sit." Samara gestured to the couches. Once they were both sitting, she looked awkwardly at Hannah. She didn't really think she had any right to ask, but she had to know. "I know about what happened to you two. Was that why you and Tom got divorced?"

"Yeah, it was," Hannah said quietly. "I felt like a victim, and I felt like Tom saw me as a victim who needed saving."

"Because you were ..." she paused, not even liking to think the word let alone say it, "raped?"

Hannah nodded. "Tom thought he should have been able to stop it from happening, but I just wanted to find a way to move on."

That was exactly how she felt.

What had happened to her had controlled her for long enough, now she wanted to put it behind her.

"How did you move on?" Samara asked.

"At first, I put all my focus on to work, building up my store. I thought if I kept busy and never thought about it, it would help me forget about what happened. And I guess in a way it did. But really, I was just existing. I wasn't really living, I wasn't happy, I wasn't moving on I was just trying to pretend that it had never happened. When Tom came back into my life, and we got remarried, that was when I finally was able to let it go. Not completely, I know that it's not something you ever get over, but Tom makes me happy, and I had to decide that that was what I wanted. I had to decide that I wasn't going to let being a rape victim define me. It's not easy, I still think about it sometimes, and occasionally I have nightmares, but every time I kiss my husband, or hold my daughter in my arms, or put my hand on my stomach and think of the baby that's growing there, I'm able to put my rape in the background and my family and my future in the front."

"Without Tom and your family do you think you would have been able to move on as you have?"

"Yes, but it would have been different. For me having Tom there made it easier. He lived through that nightmare with me, and having his support was what I needed, but I also like to think I would have gotten to where I wanted to be on my own too, it just might have taken me a little longer. Life is hard sometimes, what happened to me was horrific. I'm guessing whatever happened to you was as well, but you still have a lot ahead of you if you don't fight it. Michael loves you, and you can have everything you've ever wanted with him."

Hannah was right.

Nothing could change what her grandfather had done to her, and nothing could erase it, but if she wanted to be happy she could be, she just had to give herself permission.

"I'm not quite ready to talk about what happened to me yet, and I know I haven't really said much of anything, but still I'd appreciate it if you didn't say anything to anyone," she said to Hannah. She didn't want Fin finding out.

"Of course." Hannah reached over and squeezed her hand. "I'm sorry about whatever you went through, but I'm glad you're in a place where you're able to start putting it behind you."

"Thanks."

"Cookies for everyone, delivered by airplane," Michael called out as he came through the door with Noelle in one arm and Asher in the other. Both children held a paper plate of cookies in their hands, and both were laughing delightedly.

Samara couldn't help but smile. Michael was so good with kids, he must have been an amazing father to Heidi, and one day he might be an amazing father again to their children. This could be them a couple of years from now, sitting in their home, playing with their children. She wanted to give her children a real home, a home like she had never had with a family that was always there for them, that wasn't going to walk away. She never wanted her children to experience the pain of being unwanted, and she prayed that she never felt that pain again.

11:48 A.M.

"I better get these guys home for lunch," Hannah said.

"Okay," Samara said, trying to hide her disappointment. She'd had fun playing with Asher and Noelle. The toddlers were so bubbly and full of energy and curious about life that even the couple of tantrums they'd thrown hadn't made their time any less fun. They'd read books, and Michael had shown them all how to make goop from corn flour and water, and the kids had loved it. It had made a huge mess all over her kitchen floor, but she didn't care, the smiles of delight on the children's faces more than made up for it. Messes could be cleaned, but moments like this were gone before you even realized it.

"Aunt Sami?" Asher tugged at her skirt.

"Yeah?"

"No Cwismas twee," he said, looking confused.

"You're right," she said, picking him up. "I don't have a Christmas tree."

"Why?" Noelle asked, trying to climb up onto the couch beside her.

Samara picked Noelle up and held both toddlers on her lap. "Well, I guess I never thought Christmas was any fun because I never really had anyone to celebrate it with me."

"Why?" Asher asked.

"You guys and your whys." She laughed, not wanting to ruin her good mood with thoughts of her depressing childhood. And who knows, maybe those days were behind her now. Maybe now that she had Michael, Christmas wouldn't be so bad.

Samara looked up to see Michael watching her with a smile on his handsome face. Maybe everything would be better now that she had him.

"Okay, you two, say goodbye," Hannah instructed.

"Bye-bye," Asher crooned obediently, kissing her cheek with his sticky lips.

"Bye-bye," Noelle echoed, kissing her other cheek.

"Bye," she said, kissing the tops of both little heads. "Here you go," she said, handing Noelle to her mother. She took the coat Hannah handed her, slipped it onto Asher, then put on his beanie and mittens. "All dressed for the cold," she said when she was done, setting him on his feet.

"Love you," Asher said, wrapping a little arm around her leg and squeezing.

"I love you too, buddy." Samara felt tears pricking the backs of her eyes. She had spent so long pretending that she was okay with being alone and it was so nice to admit the truth to herself and others. She loved her brother's son, she always had, but somehow what she felt for him today was so much stronger than it had been before.

"Come on, you two, let's get you in the car." Hannah balanced her daughter on one hip, the baby bag over the other shoulder, and took Asher's hand with her free one.

"Want some help?" Michael asked.

"Sure, if you don't mind," Hannah said gratefully.

"Not at all, come here, little man." Michael scooped Asher up, and Samara followed them all to the front door. "Stay in here," Michael instructed. "Just in case he's out there somewhere watching the house."

She nodded and stood in the doorway as Michael and Hannah walked to the car in the driveway and strapped the kids into their car seats. Even though it was only lunchtime it was dull out, another gray and overcast day, more snow was fluttering through the air adding to the foot or so that already blanketed the world. All the other houses in her block had Christmas trees visible through front windows. Bright displays of Santas in sleighs, reindeer, snowmen, penguins, and polar bears decorated front lawns, and fairy lights outlined houses and their windows and front porches.

The whole world was Christmassy it seemed.

Logically, Samara knew that wasn't true, she wasn't the only person who didn't like Christmas. There were those who couldn't afford to celebrate and those who didn't want to for whatever reasons, but around here, it seemed like everyone had dressed up themselves, their children, and their homes for the holidays except her.

Was it too late to decorate?

At least put up a tree or something?

The children's whys kept running through her head, and right now, she actually couldn't think of a reason why she shouldn't make her house look Christmassy too.

"What are you thinking about?" Michael asked as he wrapped an arm around her waist and drew her to him.

"About what Asher asked," she replied as they both waved to Hannah and the kids as they drove off down the street.

"Why you don't have a Christmas tree?" he asked as he led her inside and closed and locked the door behind them. "You don't have to have a tree just because your nephew asked about it. It's okay that you don't like Christmas and it's okay if you never do. He's just curious because he's a toddler and they notice everything and they want to learn. His house has a tree and most other people's he's been to do as well, so he just wonders why you don't."

"I know." She nodded. She knew how kids' minds worked. "But I want to."

"You want to what?" Michael's hands rested on her shoulders and kneaded gently.

"I want to have a Christmas tree. I can't pretend that I can instantly start loving Christmas, but I think I could start out with a tree and then go from there. One day if we have kids, I want them to love Christmas. Oh," she stammered when she realized what she had said. "I ... uh ... sorry ... that slipped out ... I don't ... I mean ... uh ... we never talked about that ... actually, we never talked about anything ... and I ... uh ... I don't even know ..."

Michael finally took mercy on her and broke off her embarrassed rambling by curling a hand around the back of her neck and drawing her mouth to his, kissing her like he never wanted to let her go. "I want to have kids with you too," he murmured against her lips when he finished kissing her.

"Good." She smiled, glad they were on the same page. "Tomorrow is Christmas Eve. Is it too late to go and get a tree?" Since she had never had a Christmas tree before she really had no idea how or when you were supposed to get one.

"It's not too late." Michael grinned, grabbing her hand and pulling her through the foyer to the sunroom.

"Don't we need to go out to get a tree?" she asked.

"Nope." He opened her backdoor and went to the Colorado Blue Spruce, picking it up and bringing it to her. "This is perfect."

Samara laughed. "You did say it looked like a Christmas tree."

"We can put some of the popcorn strings on it, they're bright and colorful and will make it look all Christmassy."

"What about a star for the top?" she asked as they both went back inside.

"We could make one out of foil," Michael suggested, taking a string of popcorn and winding it around and around the little Christmas tree until it was spaced out evenly from top to bottom.

"You have an idea for everything."

"I have an idea of what we could be doing right now." He wiggled her eyebrows at her suggestively.

"Oh?" she feigned confusion. "Yeah? What?"

"Something upstairs." He set the bonsai tree down and dragged her up against his chest, kissing her again. This time the kiss was full of heat and passion. "I think I remember someone being a little impatient last night and not taking to the slow and tender approach too kindly. Maybe we can have a do-over."

"I like the sound of that," Samara said, her body already burning to have Michael inside it.

He took her hand and was just dragging her toward the stairs when her phone beeped with a message.

They both froze.

In an effort to try and prevent the stalker from getting hold of her current phone number only a handful of people had it. Michael had it, so did Fin, and her bosses Brady, Ryan, and Paige.

But that was it.

None of them would be calling her right now because any activity on their phones that was connected to her phone would be like bread-crumbs leading the stalker right to her.

Although it seemed like those precautions had been unnecessary.

She yanked herself out of Michael's grip and ran toward the counter where her phone sat.

"Don't look at it, Samara," Michael said, but she had already snatched up the phone and seen what was on the screen.

On it was a message much like the one Michael had received the day before.

'If they don't let you come to me then I'll go after the people they love'.

Accompanying the message was a photo.

Of Hannah carrying Noelle and Asher up the driveway toward her house.

They were wearing the same clothes they'd been in when they were here just ten minutes ago.

The stalker was at her friend's house.

He was already *inside* the house.

Her stalker was going to kill her nephew.

~

11:58 A.M.

She was really tired.

Hannah didn't remember being this tired last time around. Maybe it was because she hadn't really had a decent night's sleep since her daughter was born almost two and a half years ago. Noelle wasn't a good sleeper. She often woke at least once during the night, and ever since they'd moved her from a crib to a bed, she usually came to their room and spent the rest of the night in bed with her and Tom.

That was why naptime was so important.

Noelle usually had a good hour nap in the afternoon, particularly if she'd had a busy morning, and the kids had had a great time visiting with Samara and Michael. Michael was great with kids, which was no surprise since he'd had a daughter who had died, and even Samara had ended up relaxing and just having fun. It looked like Michael would be good for Samara, and Hannah was glad that Samara was finally in a place where she was ready to try to let her past stay in the past.

"What do you guys want for lunch?" she asked as she carried both toddlers toward the front door.

"Hot cheese sandwich," Noelle replied immediately. Her daughter was obsessed with grilled cheese sandwiches, some days she had them for breakfast, lunch, and dinner.

"Chicky nuggies," Asher squealed. She looked after her husband's partner's little boy two days a week, and every single time she had him and asked what he wanted for lunch he said chicken nuggets.

"I think we can manage some grilled cheese sandwiches and chicken nuggets," she said. Setting the two children down on the porch, she rifled through her bag for the keys she'd dropped in there when she'd gotten the kids out. If she put them down in the driveway, they were only going to go running off, chasing each other across the lawn, and she wasn't in the mood to go running after them. She wanted to get lunch done, then she'd read a few stories and tuck Noelle and Asher in, then she might go and have a lie-down.

"Cookies?" Noelle asked hopefully.

"I don't think so, honey, you already had some at Samara's house. As soon as we get inside, I want you two to take your shoes, coats, mittens, and beanies off and leave them all by the front door," she instructed as she found the key and slid it into the lock. She liked the kids to be as independent as possible, so she always had them do what they could on their own.

"Okay," both children agreed.

"Inside," she shepherded them inside when she pushed the door open, then pulled it behind her and locked it, then sagged against it. As much as she would love to lie down right now, she had to get through lunch first. Then this afternoon after they had all had a sleep the kids could help her bake cookies which she and Noelle would put out for Santa on Christmas Eve. Even before she'd had her daughter, she had left out cookies on Christmas Eve, it was a tradition from her childhood she hadn't been able to let go of. She loved sharing the tradition with her daughter and couldn't wait to share it with this new little baby as well.

She rested a hand on her small baby bump. In five months, their lives would change forever. It was exciting and a little scary. Dealing with one child was one thing, but dealing with a newborn and a fiercely independent toddler was another. But two children meant twice as many kisses and cuddles, twice as many giggles and games, and twice as much love. They'd figure out how to deal with the practicalities just like they had the first time around.

"Great job, guys," she said when she saw that Noelle and Asher had done as she asked. "Now run on through to the living room and play while I make lunch."

The kids ran off, and Hannah pushed herself away from the door, only another hour or so until she could take a quick nap. If she threw on a load of laundry while she made lunch, then she could sleep a little longer. If she was lucky, then maybe the kids would sleep for two hours; sometimes they did when they were really tired.

Hannah was walking down the hall to the kitchen when her phone rang. She nearly ignored it because she was thinking about getting a jump start on dinner while she made lunch but thought better of it. If it was Tom calling to check in like he sometimes did, he'd only worry if she didn't answer.

When she pulled her phone from her bag she saw Michael's name on the screen, not her husband's. She must have left something at Samara's house. Whatever it was it could stay there, she wasn't dragging the kids back to the car, strapping them in, driving all the way there, then back here again. She'd still have to make them lunch, and they'd be late getting down for their naps, and she wouldn't have a chance to put a load of laundry on and start dinner, so she wouldn't be able to lie down and nap while the kids napped.

"Hey, Michael, whatever we left Tom will pick up on—"

"Grab the kids and get out of the house," Michael's frantic voice interrupted her.

"What?" she asked, confused. She was tired and was sure she hadn't heard him correctly.

"He's in the house," Michael said. "The stalker. He just sent Samara a photo of you carrying the kids in from the car. The photo was taken from inside. Get Noelle and Asher and get out. We called the cops, and Tom, Samara, and I are on our way, but he's already there, just get out, go to a neighbor's house."

She didn't listen to anything else.

Just shoved her phone into her pocket and ran to the living room.

Hannah skidded to a stop when she came through the door.

A man around her age stood in the living room with Asher in his arms.

He also had a gun.

She had a paralyzing phobia of guns.

Even the sight of one was enough to have her go basically into a trance.

But she couldn't do that right now.

Her daughter's life depended on her holding it together.

Help was coming, she just had to keep the man here and talking until then.

"Noelle, come to mommy," she ordered her daughter. Reading the tone in her voice, Noelle immediately ran over. Grabbing her daughter, she shoved her out of the room. "Go to your room. Now." Noelle looked like she wanted to cry, but instead she did as she was told, and Hannah said a quick prayer of thanks that her usually stubborn daughter had for once done as she was asked without trying to argue or negotiate. With her daughter out of the way, she just had to find a way to get herself and Asher away from the stalker. "Put him down," she said, trying to infuse into her voice confidence she didn't feel.

"Don't do anything stupid," the man warned. "I don't want to hurt you or your daughter. I just need to take Samara's nephew so they stop trying to keep us apart. I won't do anything to hurt him. When they give me Samara, I'll give him back."

"He's scared. Please, just give him to me, and you can stay here and wait for Samara. She's coming. She wouldn't want you to hurt Asher, she loves him. I was going to make the kids grilled cheese sandwiches and chicken nuggets for lunch. I can make some for you as well, then we can just sit at the table and wait for Samara to get here, then we can sort all of this out."

For a moment it looked like he was going to do as she said, but then he shook his head. "I don't think so. You seem nice, but the others aren't. They don't want Samara and me to be happy. Everything will be okay." He said it like he truly meant to console her, but nothing was okay. This man was here in her home, and he had a gun. "Just stay right there, and when they come tell them I won't hurt the kid so long as they let Samara come to me," the stalker said.

There was no way she could stand back and let this man just walk out of here with Asher. The little boy was squirming, trying to get out of the man's arms, he wasn't crying yet, but his big brown eyes were watery. "Please, just give him to me."

"Stand back," the man's eyes grew dark, and he raised the gun pointing it directly at her. Her entire body was shaking violently, and she could barely focus on anything other than the barrel of the gun.

"I can't let you take him." She tried to tear her gaze away from the gun but couldn't.

He muttered something under his breath, then stalked toward her.

She screamed, sure he was about to kill her, her unborn child, and then her daughter before fleeing with Asher.

The man reached her, standing right in front of her. She tried to reach for Asher, hoping to tear him from the man's arms.

The butt of the gun swung down, connecting with the side of her head.

The blow stunned her, her vision went cloudy, and she dropped to her knees as the world spun wildly around her.

Another blow struck her in the back of the head, and she fell into unconsciousness.

~

12:08 P.M.

"You don't leave my sight for a second," Michael ordered as they pulled up in front of Hannah's house.

Samara nodded, much too vigorously, hurting her neck.

"I mean it," Michael added.

"Okay," Samara said because she knew he wanted a verbal acknowledgment. He hadn't wanted her to come. In fact, he had all but handcuffed her to the off-duty cop who had been helping out and watching her house. But she had to come here. This all happening because of her, and she wasn't going to be sidelined anymore.

Just as they climbed out of the car, another car came screeching to a stop half in the street half in the driveway.

A frantic Tom and Chloe jumped out, and she and Michael jogged up to meet them.

"Do we know anything?" Tom demanded.

"Just what I told you on the phone. That the stalker was inside the house when Hannah got back and said he was taking Asher unless we gave him Samara," Michael answered.

Chloe's face paled further, and Samara felt her panic amp up a notch.

This was all her fault.

Because of her, her brother might lose his son.

Fin and Chloe had already lost one child when he was born too prematurely after a car accident, and now they might lose another.

Or they might have already lost Asher.

They didn't know if the stalker was still here or if he had already fled.

"Let's just get in there," Chloe snapped, her gun in hand and a look on her face that said she welcomed the chance to use it.

"Stay behind me," Michael instructed as the four of them made their way toward the front door.

Samara stayed as close to Michael's back as she could without actually climbing on it and prayed that they had gotten here in time. If the stalker was still here, they could arrest him, and this would all be over. If they were too late and he was already gone with her nephew, then she would never forgive herself, and her brother would never forgive her either.

Tom opened the door; the house was quiet. Was that a good sign or a bad one?

Painstakingly slowly they crept through the house until they got to the living room.

Where they found Hannah lying unmoving on the floor.

Tom ran to her, dropping to his knees at his wife's side and pressing his fingers to her neck. "She's alive," he told them, his voice thick with emotion.

"Stay here with Tom, I'll check the rest of the house," Michael told her.

Michael and Chloe disappeared, and Samara stood awkwardly in the middle of the room and watched as Tom gathered Hannah up and carried her to the couch, laying her down and grabbing a blanket from the back of the couch to spread over her.

"He's gone," Chloe half-sobbed as she came running back into the room.

"Noelle was in her room." Michael held the little girl in his arms as he followed Chloe into the living room and handed the child to her. "You take her, I'll go get some towels for Hannah's head."

"Chloe?" Fin's voice called out, and a moment later he appeared in the doorway.

"He's gone," Chloe sobbed, throwing her arms around her husband. "Asher is gone. We were too late. I'm so sorry."

"It's not your fault," Fin said, dragging Chloe closer and crushing her against him.

Her brother was right.

This wasn't Chloe's fault.

Or Tom's, or Hannah's, or Michael's, or anyone else's.

It was her fault.

Hers and hers alone.

"We'll get him back," Fin told Chloe, whose head nodded against his shoulder.

On the couch, Hannah groaned, and everyone's attention snapped to her.

"Hannah?" Tom asked, brushing gently at his wife's hair, freeing a lock of it from where it was stuck in the blood that had flowed from her head wound down her face.

"Noelle?" she asked, bolting upright.

"She's fine," Tom soothed. "She's right there."

"Asher?" Hannah asked, holding out her arms toward her daughter, and Samara carried the little girl over to her mom.

"He's gone," Tom told her.

"I'm so sorry," Hannah cried, clutching her child close.

"It is not your fault. You shouldn't be moving about so much. You were hit over the head and passed out when we found you." Tom moved from where he had been kneeling beside the couch to sit beside his wife, pulling her and Noelle onto his lap.

Hannah didn't look appeased and shifted her gaze to Fin and Chloe. "I'm so sorry. I tried to stop him."

"Shh." Tom stroked his wife's hair, his face a stark white as he realized how close he had come to losing his whole family.

"It's okay, Hannah." Chloe straightened herself and came to sit on the couch beside Tom and Hannah. "Tom's right, it isn't your fault. Did he say anything? Anything that might tell us where he took Asher?"

"He said that he didn't want to hurt me and that he wouldn't hurt Asher. He said he would just keep him until you let him have Samara," Hannah said. She was pale, and she looked like she was in pain, she rested her head on her husband's shoulder and closed her eyes.

"An ambulance is going to be here soon," Tom told her.

Michael returned and handed the towels to Tom, who pressed one to the bloody spot on the back of Hannah's head.

This was just more of what they already knew.

The stalker wasn't going to stop until he had her.

Why were they making this any harder than it had to be?

How many more people were they going to let him hurt or kill? Were they just going to sit by and watch him kill her two-year-old nephew?

Sirens sounded, and a minute later the room filled with cops and paramedics. Everyone seemed to be busy, everyone seemed to have something to do except for her. Samara just stood in the middle of the room, surrounded by the hubbub but feeling more alone than she had ever felt as a child.

The look on her brother's face had her feeling like someone had doused sulfuric acid all over her and it was eating her away bit by bit.

She couldn't do this any longer.

She couldn't just stand by, safe and protected, while everyone she loved and strangers on the street were in danger.

"What are we going to do?" Chloe's voice penetrated the panicked haze that had descended on her. Chloe sounded terrified and angry and a million other things. Fin had his hands on her shoulders and was trying to calm her down, but he looked just as close to falling apart as his wife did.

Her phone buzzed, and Samara knew before she even pulled it from her purse who it was going to be.

She was right.

On the screen was a message from the same number that had sent the picture of Hannah and the kids. The message was short—just an address. But he hadn't needed to say more. She knew what he meant. If she went to the address he had given her, then he would let her nephew go and take her instead.

This could be the break they needed.

If she went to meet him wearing a wire and with the cops tailing her but remaining out of sight, then he would think that he'd gotten what he wanted. He'd let Asher go, and Chloe and Tom could arrest him.

Samara went to her brother and tugged on his arm. "Fin."

"Not now, Samara," he said, shrugging her off.

"But," she started.

"I said not now." Fin spun around to face her, his expression unlike anything she had ever seen on her big brother before. He hated her. It was her fault that his son was missing and in danger. Of course he hated her. She was stupid to have believed anything else.

"Sorry," she murmured, releasing her grip and retreating. No one was paying any attention to her. Tom was holding Noelle on his hip and hovering over Hannah who was being lifted onto a stretcher. Fin and Chloe were clinging to each other and answering questions from a cop. Michael was in the corner speaking with another cop. Other cops bustled about, and a crime scene unit was carrying cases in.

No one would notice if she just slipped away.

She loved Michael, and she didn't want to do anything to hurt him, but saving her nephew was more important.

Quietly, she slipped from the room.

It was better this way.

～

12:34 P.M.

·  ·  ·

Dante couldn't wipe the smile off his face.

Finally, he'd done it.

And this time it was going to work.

This time he wasn't going to scare her, making her jump out of the car. No one was going to come between them, no one was going to keep her from him. They were going to be together forever.

He couldn't wait for her to get here.

It shouldn't be long now. He had texted her the address almost ten minutes ago, and he was only just a couple of blocks from her friend Hannah Drake's house.

He couldn't sit still. He was like a little kid on Christmas morning, squirming and wriggling like he had ants in his pants.

"Juice peese."

The voice startled him.

For a moment he had forgotten he wasn't alone.

Dante turned in his seat to see Asher Patrick sitting on the backseat of his car. The toddler had been very well behaved, he'd cried a little at first, but as soon as he'd given the little boy a toy train and something to eat, he'd settled down.

"Here's your juice," Dante said, passing it over. "Be careful though, don't spill it."

It wasn't that he didn't like kids because he did, and he wanted to have babies with Samara, but he didn't like cleaning up after children. They were messy and dirty and always sticky. When they had kids, they were getting a live-in nanny to look after them.

"Tank oo," the little boy said as he took his juice. The child was very polite, and he was glad he wouldn't have to hurt him.

All morning he hadn't known exactly what he was going to do today, who he was going to go after. He had thought about setting a bomb under the car of the FBI Agents who were trying to find him. Then he'd considered the possibility of shooting out one of their tires, so they crashed the car. The idea of blowing up the building where the private security firm that Samara worked for was located had also crossed his mind. He had been about to settle on that idea as it would not only get them to let Samara go but would also punish them for getting between him and Samara.

But then he realized that if he hurt the people that Samara loved and cared about it would only wind up hurting her. Killing strangers was one thing, but one of the FBI Agents was Samara's sister-in-law, and the other was a friend, and the people she worked with were also friends.

Then the idea to take Samara's nephew occurred to him. Just long enough to make everyone realize that he wasn't going anywhere until he got what he wanted. And soon he would have it. Then they could drop the kid off and drive up to the cabin.

Movement in his side mirror caught his attention, and someone knocked on the driver's door.

"Samara." He grinned and threw it open. As much as he wanted to jump out and throw his arms around her, he had to be cautious, very aware that the FBI might be trying to lure him into a trap. "Are you alone? Are they following you?"

"I'm alone," she replied.

Unable to hold back any longer, Dante sprung from the car, wrapped his arms around her waist, and lifted her feet off the ground, spinning her around in a circle, then setting her back down. He took her face between his hands and stared into her gorgeous blue eyes. He had been waiting for this moment for so long that it didn't feel real. Slowly, he dipped his head and kissed Samara, her lips were warm and soft, and she tasted sweet like candy.

This was heaven.

Samara didn't kiss him back. He would have been hurt, but he knew she was just worried about her nephew. He loved that she loved the little boy so much.

"He's okay," Dante assured her. "See." He pointed to the backseat. "I got him grilled cheese and chicken nuggets for lunch because that was what your friend Hannah was going to give him. I also gave him a Christmas cookie, I hope that was okay," he said anxiously, he didn't want to have done the wrong thing, and some people were particular about small children eating too much sugar.

"Th-that's fine." Samara nodded. "Can I pick him up?"

"Of course."

Samara wrenched open the back door and snatched the child up, clutching him tightly against her chest and burying her face in his messy brown hair. "You okay, sweetheart?"

"Want Mommy," Asher replied.

"I know, baby, you miss your mommy. But it's okay, she's going to be here real soon, right?" Samara looked at him.

"I'm not going to hurt him. I didn't hurt your friend or her little girl, did I?" he reminded her. Those FBI agents and the bodyguards had her so brainwashed. He didn't want to hurt people, he wasn't a killer. He had been backed into a corner and done what he needed to do.

"Thank you for not hurting Hannah and Noelle," Samara said.

"You're welcome. We'll leave the kid here and then I have a surprise for you."

"It's cold out and snowing, and he's not wearing a coat or mittens or a beanie. Can't we drop him off somewhere? Maybe in front of a store or even just leave him on the nearest front porch, ring the doorbell, and run? Please," she added like she thought he was going to tell her no.

She didn't get it yet.

All her life she had been abandoned, people had walked out on her, she thought he was going to do the same thing, but she was wrong.

He was never going anywhere.

It was the two of them together for life, that was what he wanted, and he knew it was what she wanted as well.

"We can do that, sweetheart," he told her. "Anything you want. I just want to make you happy."

Samara looked at him oddly, like she wasn't sure what to make of him yet. His beautiful girl would understand soon, she was his princess, and he wanted to make all her dreams come true.

"Let's take him up to that house and leave him there, I see a light on, and there's a car in the drive, so we know someone is home," Dante said. "You get in the car, and I'll make the drop. We'll need to get out of here as quickly as we can, I don't want anyone trying to take you away from me again."

"Maybe I should take him," Samara suggested.

Dante shook his head. He couldn't risk the homeowner answering the door too quickly and seeing her. If they tried to call the cops thinking she was abandoning her son, that would ruin everything, and he would hate to have to kill someone in front of Samara and her nephew. "I'll do it," he said, holding out his hands to take the child. "Give him here."

Somewhat reluctantly, Samara passed him over, giving him one last kiss on the top of the head before she completely released her hold on him.

"You get in the car; you're not dressed properly to be out in the cold either."

He watched to make sure that Samara did as he'd asked and got inside the car. Once she had, he carried the child toward the house he was parked in front of.

"Aunt Sami," Asher called out, trying to get out of his arms and back to his aunt. The little boy would no doubt miss Samara, but in time he would get over it. And who knows, maybe one day when her family and friends realized that he and Samara loved one another they might come around, and then Samara could have it all, him and her family.

"Stay here like a good little boy and drink the rest of your juice and your mommy will be here soon," he instructed the child as he set him down on the doorstep. Dante reached up and pressed the doorbell, then quickly ran down the path past a blow-up Santa and Rudolph and jumped into the car where Samara was waiting for him.

As he shoved the key into the ignition, he saw a woman come running down the path, Asher in her arms.

He wasn't getting stopped now, not when they were almost home free.

Dante stomped on the gas, and the car lurched off down the street.

The nightmare was over, he had Samara, and now their fairytale happily ever after ending could begin.

～

1:00 P.M.

.  .  .

All Michael wanted to do was wrap Samara up in his arms, feel her warm breath against his neck, breathe in the scent of her lavender shampoo, and center himself.

The last twenty-four hours had been a rollercoaster ride of emotions. From making love to Samara for the first time, to playing with Noelle and Asher and thinking how wonderful it would be to have a child around again, to rushing over here in a panic when they got the stalker's message and arriving to find Hannah unconscious and Asher gone. If it wasn't for Samara, he would be craving a drink right about now.

He'd been busy talking with the cops and his boss as they tried to figure out what their next move would be. Tom had taken Noelle, and they'd gone in the ambulance with Hannah to the hospital, and Chloe was basically paralyzed with fear about her son, so he had been catching the local cops up as best he could on the case and what they knew so far.

Which wasn't a lot.

The best they could hope for was that the stalker would make contact with Samara again and give her directions on where to meet up with him. Then they could follow her and arrest the stalker and hopefully this would all be over by the end of the day, then they could all relax and enjoy Christmas.

Michael froze as he stepped into the living room.

Samara wasn't there.

Although he fought against the knowledge, he knew instinctively where she was.

The stalker had already contacted her, and she'd slipped away to meet him.

His eyes hadn't caught on yet and still scanned the room as though Samara had simply turned invisible, and if he kept looking, sooner or later, she would show up. His gaze landed on Samara's brother. When he'd gone to talk with the cops, he'd told Fin to keep an eye on Samara, worried that she was about ready to cave under the pressure.

"Where's Samara?" he asked, storming over to Fin.

"Over there somewhere." Fin didn't even turn around, just tossed a hand up in the air pointing behind him.

"No, she's not. I asked you to keep an eye on her." He knew that

Samara was holding on by a thread. The only reason he hadn't remained glued to her side was because he'd told her brother to watch her and not let her out of his sight.

"I'm trying to calm my wife down, she's a mess." Fin threw a glare over his shoulder.

"So is your sister. I asked you to watch her, and now she's gone."

"What's the big deal? She's probably outside getting some fresh air."

"She better be," Michael muttered.

He turned and ran outside. The street was abuzz with activity, the FBI's ERT unit was scouring the house, as was the local crime scene unit, cops were canvassing the neighbors, there were people everywhere, but no Samara.

She was gone.

They'd driven here in his car, and it was still parked where he'd left it, so wherever the stalker had told Samara to meet him it had to be close by because she would have gone on foot.

"Hey," he called to the nearest cop. "Did you see Samara Patrick leave this house?"

"A woman with dark hair went walking up the street that way." The young woman pointed. "I didn't see her face, but it could have been Ms. Patrick."

"How long ago?"

"Fifteen minutes maybe."

That was plenty of time to get wherever she was going, she could already be with the stalker.

"Start searching the streets within a ten-block perimeter," he ordered.

If they were lucky, Samara and the stalker were still nearby.

If they were unlucky, they were already on the way to wherever the stalker intended to keep Samara.

"She's not out there," he screamed as he ran back into the living room. "She's gone. This is your fault." He pointed at Fin.

"Calm down, let's not make this worse than it already is," his boss Brady Crowley, said in what Michael was sure was meant to be a soothing tone. "Fin's son is missing."

"And now so is Samara. She gave herself to her stalker to get Asher back because she's still trying to make up for the suicide attempt when she was thirteen. She thinks you're still angry with her for doing it." He glowered at Fin who was right at this moment the target for all the fear swarming inside him.

"I am," Fin shot back, fear no doubt spurring him on as well. "We had the same childhood, we had the same people walk out on us, and I never tried to end my life. I never gave up on Samara, but she gave up on me."

The words were out of his mouth before he could stop them even though he knew he had promised Samara he wouldn't tell her brother the truth about her suicide attempt. "Your parents and grandfather leaving weren't why she did it. Your grandfather was abusing her. She was thirteen years old and felt all alone with no one to turn to for help, so she did the only thing she felt she could do, and you've been punishing her for it for the last fifteen years."

Fin paled dramatically and swayed enough that Chloe stepped up and wrapped an arm around his waist. "What?"

"She has spent the last fifteen years trying to make up for what she did because you wouldn't forgive her for it. She didn't do anything wrong, but you made her feel like she did, so now she feels like she has to be perfect and maybe that will get you to forgive her. She's gone, and we still don't even know the stalker's name. He has her, he's going to take her and disappear, and we might never get her back." Michael had never wanted a drink so badly in his life. If they didn't find Samara, he could easily foresee how the rest of his life would turn out. He'd drink himself into oblivion until death finally released him from hell on earth.

"I didn't know," Fin said softly, his face devastated.

"She didn't want you to know."

"Why?"

"Probably because she doesn't think you'd care," he spat back. He needed to do something that helped him control his overwhelming need to drink and lashing out at Fin was achieving that.

"I love my sister. I always loved her. I was hurt because I thought she wanted to leave me as well, but I never stopped loving her. Before she disappeared, she wanted to tell me something, but I brushed her off because I was only focused on Chloe. She was going to tell me that the stalker contacted her again."

Fin was no doubt correct.

If he had just listened to what Samara wanted to tell him, then she never would have walked out of this house determined to sacrifice herself to save Asher.

Before he could say anything else, Brady jumped in, "We just got a report of an abandoned toddler matching Asher's description about four blocks from here. Apparently, someone left him on the front porch, rang the bell, then ran off. We know Samara left here to meet the stalker, so he had no reason to keep Asher."

"Let's go," Chloe said, already running toward the door.

No one spoke as the four of them piled into Brady's car and made the two-minute drive to the house where the toddler had been left. As much as Michael hoped that it was Asher and that the child was safe, if the stalker had left him behind, then that meant he had what he wanted.

Samara.

She was now in the hands of a violent man who had killed to try to get her. When he realized that Samara didn't love him, he would wind up killing her too.

"Asher." Chloe sobbed as Brady parked the car and she caught sight of her son. Both she and Fin flung their doors open and jumped out, and Chloe snatched up the little boy and clutched him tight. "Are you okay, baby?"

"Mama, too tight," the child said, squirming in his mother's arms, seemingly unfazed by the ordeal he'd been through.

"He's okay, he's okay," Fin murmured over and over again, as much to reassure himself as his wife Michael suspected. He wrapped his arms around his wife and son and the three of them stood together, reunited, and happy. This nightmare was over for them, but it wasn't for Michael, and it definitely wasn't for Samara.

Brady went to speak with the cops, and Michael stood off to the side by himself, yanking out his phone. He needed access to Samara's phone, if he could get into the GPS system, then they might be able to get a read on where she and the stalker were. His computer skills might not be as good as Samara's, but they weren't bad, and in a couple of minutes, a red dot showed up on his screen.

"I got them," he called out to Brady.

"And I got the license plate of the car the stalker is driving. The woman whose house he left Asher at was right by the door when he rang the bell. She chased after him because she knew something was wrong and made sure she got the license number," Brady said, joining him.

"Let's go." Hope surged through him. They knew what car Samara and the stalker were in, and so long as Samara kept her phone on, they would be able to trace her.

"I'm coming too," Fin announced.

"Stay with your family," Michael said dismissively. Fin was partly to blame for Samara being in danger, and he didn't want the man anywhere near him while he was teetering on the edge, barely able to keep his fear and anger under control.

"Samara is my sister, and I love her. She's in danger, and it's my fault. I'm coming with you," Fin said firmly.

He didn't want to waste any more time arguing. They could lose the signal at any moment, so Michael merely grunted and climbed into the front passenger seat. He had promised Samara that he wouldn't let her stalker hurt her and he intended to keep that promise.

1:19 P.M.

So far, they had been driving in silence.

Samara didn't know what to say to her stalker that wasn't going to make him angry. She could always try jumping out of the car again, but she suspected he wouldn't just keep driving. He would come back for her, tie her up, lock her in the trunk, or kill her on the spot. She wasn't sure, but she knew he would do something. Even if it did work, he would only start killing again to get her back, maybe go after Asher again, or her brother, or Michael.

She couldn't risk it.

This time, she was staying right where she was.

When the stalker had started harassing her, she had disabled the GPS on her phone because she hadn't wanted him to use it to find out where she lived. Obviously that had been pointless as he had figured it out anyway, but since they were good friends, she had told Michael how to enable it again remotely. Maybe subconsciously she had always known that the stalker situation was going to end badly.

Sooner or later Michael and the others were going to realize she was gone. Even if they didn't, someone would find Asher, call the cops to report an abandoned toddler, her nephew would be identified because there would already be reports of his abduction, then they would figure out that she had traded herself.

It was inevitable they would come looking for her, and Michael should know to re-enable the GPS tracking on her phone. Once he did that, they would be able to find her. All she had to do was try not to make this man angry until someone came for her.

That seemed doable.

Just sit here, keep her mouth shut, her hands folded in her lap so that he knew she wasn't a threat to him, and wait.

"I can't wait to show you the cabin," the man said, a little nervously like they were on a first date and he wanted to impress her but also not come on too strongly.

It looked like her sit here quietly and wait plan was out the window.

"I decorated it," he continued, "for Christmas. I wanted it to be special for when you came."

"Umm, thank you," Samara said. Just a few hours ago she and Michael had been decorating her bonsai Colorado Blue Spruce when she'd decided she wanted to try doing something Christmassy. Now she was pretty sure she hated Christmas even more than she had before. She didn't want to see this man's cabin, and she didn't care that he had decorated it, she just wanted to go home with Michael.

How ironic that she had finally found someone she wanted to share her life with, someone who actually made her feel safe and wanted, and who made her doubt that her suicide attempt was something she had to make up for, and now she might never get to find out what could be between them. She and Michael might have spent the rest of their lives happily married, raising kids, then enjoying retirement and grandkids, but now she could be dead before they ever had a chance.

"You're welcome." He turned his head toward her and smiled. It was a shy smile like he didn't really have much confidence in himself.

Why didn't she remember him?

They must have met somewhere before. He was too obsessed with her for them not to have had some physical contact at some point.

But where?

And when?

She had to figure out his name. How could she find out without outright asking him? He thought that she knew who he was, in all the messages he had sent her, he had never signed them with his name. If she let on that she had no idea who he was and why he was obsessed with her, it was going to make him angry.

That was the last thing she wanted.

"So, uh, thank you for looking after Asher so well," she said. He had at least been true to his word in regard to her nephew. He had let him go exactly like he'd said he would, and he'd even gone to the trouble of getting Asher the lunch that Hannah had been going to make for him.

"Of course," the man said, smiling at her again. He had a creepy smile, it was borderline insane, which fit in with his clearly delusional behavior.

"I guess one day you could be his uncle," Samara said. It was kind of lame, but she was hoping he took the bait and filled in the gap there, supplying his name. She felt like if she could just get his name, she would at least have something to work with, and right now she needed something—anything—even something small.

"Uncle Dante, I like the sound of that."

Dante.

She was sure she didn't know anyone called Dante. Samara wracked her brain trying to come up with every place she had ever been and everyone she had ever met to try to find a Dante. She came up empty. As far as she knew, she had never met a Dante. But they didn't have to have ever really come into contact for him to fixate on her.

Her trick to get him to say his name had worked. Could she be lucky a second time and get him to tell her how they'd met?

"Dante?"

"Yes?" He glanced over at her, the creepy smile still in place.

"About when we met ..."

"You're right." He nodded emphatically and reached over to take her hand. As much as she wanted to pull away from his touch, she forced herself to stay still, she couldn't afford to do anything to upset him, and he believed that she was in love with him just like he thought he was in love with her. "I haven't thanked you properly yet."

"Thanked me?"

"For saving my life." His hand squeezed hers, curling around her fingers and clinging to them like if he let her go she might disappear.

"Saved your life?" As far as she knew she had never saved anyone's life with the possible exception of trading herself for her nephew, but she knew that wasn't what Dante was talking about.

"You're so sweet, but you don't have to be modest, that night on the bridge I was going to jump. I didn't want to live anymore, but then you came along. You stopped. That was the first time in a long time that anyone had ever cared enough to even notice me let alone stop and go out of their way to help me."

Dante was the man from last summer?

Around eleven one night, she had been driving back after attending a seminar on a new malware tracking software when she'd seen a car pulled over on the side of the bridge. The car's headlights had been on, and in them, she had seen the silhouette of a man. She had assumed the man's car had broken down, so she'd stopped to ask if he had called for help or if he needed to use her cell. The man had told her that a friend was already on the way to get him but thanked her profusely for her kindness.

She had gotten back in her car, driven home, fallen into bed, and promptly forgotten all about the interaction.

Dante obviously had not.

His car hadn't been broken down, he had been going to jump off the bridge, but her gesture had convinced him that not only did he not want to die but that there was some hidden meaning behind her stopping.

It had been dark, and she'd been tired, she had never seen the man's face, but Dante must have gotten a glimpse of her license plate and used it to track her down.

"Up until that moment I wanted to die, but fate brought you to me. I was going to call you and thank you for what you did, but when I looked you up, I found out about your past. You tried to commit suicide too. I knew it was a sign. You saved me because no one had been there to save you. You saved me because you felt the connection that we had. Right here." Dante pulled the car over to the side of the road on the bridge where their lives had first crossed paths. "This is the spot. This is where our souls became one. Before we go to the cabin, I thought we might spend a moment here."

He released her hand and got out of the car, coming around to open her door for her and draw her out. Dante led her to the bridge's railing and then stood behind her, his arms wrapped around her waist, holding her tightly against his body.

Samara briefly considered ripping herself from his arms and throwing herself over the railing down into the river below. That had to be better than living the rest of her life as this man's captive, pretending to love him until she said or did something that set off his temper and he killed her.

If it wasn't for Michael, she might have done it.

But he would be looking for her, he wouldn't give up on her, and she couldn't give up on him. He had promised to keep her safe, and he'd said that he loved her, she just had to hold on to that. He was coming for her, she knew he was, just like she knew he would never stop looking for her.

"Your perfume," he murmured, "Lavender. I knew as soon as I smelled it. We're meant to be together, it's our destiny. I will love you forever, my beautiful, sweet princess. Neither of us was wanted, but from here on out, I pledge my love and loyalty to you. I am yours for all eternity, and you are mine. I won't let anyone take you away from me ever again."

She shuddered, and it had nothing to do with the snow falling on them. The only thing that was ever going to free her from Dante's grip was death.

~

1:42 P.M.

Dante was in heaven.

This was exactly what he had been dreaming about since last summer—standing with the woman he loved in his arms, surrounded by the scent of lavender, where their love affair began.

"Thank you, Samara, for saving me and for loving me," he whispered in her ear. He felt her shudder and tightened his hold. She felt it too, the powerful connection between them that had only grown now they were together.

They were going to be so happy together.

Stopping here was an important step for them, but he couldn't wait to get her to the cabin. It was only another hour away from here. They'd be there by about two-thirty if they left now, they could have a late lunch, maybe go for a walk in the snow, then they could curl up in front of the fireplace and enjoy each other's company.

"We should get back in the car, you're not wearing a coat, and it's snowing, I don't want you to get too cold." He ran his hands up and down her arms, warming her, he couldn't wait to get her home and start spoiling her. Starting with an early Christmas gift.

"Dante Sundry, let go of Samara and get down on your knees, hands behind your head."

The voice startled him, and he spun around, bringing Samara with him.

Three men stood a couple of yards away; two were armed, all three looked like they were about ready to rip his head off.

He knew who they were. One was Michael Stein, he had been living in Samara's house the last few days, the next was Samara's brother Fin Patrick, and the third was one of the owners of the private security firm Samara and Michael worked for, his name was Brady Crowley.

How had they found him?

Samara must have her phone on her, and they had used it to track her location.

Dante felt his blood boil. Why couldn't they just leave him alone? He and Samara just wanted to live their lives in peace. What was wrong with that? Why were these people so hell-bent on ruining it? Why couldn't they just let them live their lives, they weren't bothering anyone, and it was no one else's business but their own.

"Leave us alone," he shouted. "We want to be together. Why can't you understand that?"

"You killed three people, Dante," Michael said. "We can't let you do that and then just walk away."

"That was your fault. *You're* the reason they're dead because you were trying to keep us apart. But we're together now, and you're never going to take Samara away from me again." He would do whatever it took to make sure that he and Samara remained together.

"You're scaring her," Michael said. "Just let her go and we can talk about this."

"Do you think I'm an idiot?"

"No, of course not," Brady said.

"Well, you must if you think that I believe that the second I let Samara go you're not going to shoot me." He hated being treated like an idiot. He wasn't. Not even close, his IQ was off the charts.

"It doesn't have to go down that way," Brady said. "Cops are going to be here any minute. You can give yourself up quietly, no one here wants to shoot you. Nor does anyone want Samara to get hurt accidentally. I know you don't. You love her, right?"

"Are you questioning my love for Samara?" he screamed, dragging her closer and holding her so tight he heard her sharp intake of air as his arm crushed her chest. Immediately he loosened his hold a little.

"No," Brady answered calmly. "No one is questioning that you love Samara. We've all seen what you've done to try to get to her. You love her just like you loved Lavender."

His whole body turned to ice at the mention of the name.

*Her* name.

The name of the girl he had loved as a child.

"Her mother killed her, and so you killed her," Brady continued.

"Stop it," he yelled. He didn't want to hear this right now. He didn't want to think about his past, not today on what was supposed to be the happiest day of his life. He was supposed to enjoy having Samara in his arms, he was supposed to be taking her home and making love to her for the first time. This day was supposed to be perfect, and once again, these men were ruining it.

"Lavender's mother was your nanny, right? An only child, your parents were hardly ever home. Most of the time it was just the two of you at that huge, secluded estate. Just the two of you. No one to stop her from hurting you. She used to lock you out of the house when it was snowing, she would blindfold you and make you take off all of your clothes and wash in the snow. She lied to you, Dante, her daughter was already dead before she became your nanny."

Lies.

That was lies.

He knew that for a fact.

Lavender hadn't been dead, he'd talked to her, touched her, kissed her. She was flesh and bones, as real as he was.

"Nice try, but I know that Lavender was alive, so stop playing games and let us go," Dante said.

"Lavender died before you were born," Brady said. "Her mother did to her the same things that she did to you. She stripped her daughter naked and left her out in the snow, only one night she fell asleep, and by the time she woke up, it was already too late. Lavender was dead. Victoria was arrested, but she suffered a psychotic break. She developed a split personality, she took on her daughter's identity as well as her own. When you thought it was Lavender that you were talking to it was really her mother. Victoria served sixteen years in a psychiatric hospital for her daughter's death, then when she was released, she remarried and changed her name. Your parents didn't know who she was, who they were hiring to raise their child for them."

They could keep lying to him, but it didn't make any of this true.

And what they were saying couldn't be true.

He knew it wasn't.

He had proof.

He carried it with him everywhere.

"Lavender wrote me a note. The day she committed suicide, she left it along with a lock of her hair in our special place."

"Did you ever actually see Lavender?" Brady asked.

"Her mother hurt her, that's why she committed suicide. But when Victoria would lock me out in the snow Lavender would come, we'd talk, and when we got older, sometimes we would kiss."

"But she would always blindfold you, wouldn't she?" Brady persisted.

"They sounded different," he insisted. "They smelled different. Lavender always smelled of lavender, Victoria didn't."

"I'm sorry, Dante, but Lavender died when she was thirteen, two years before you were born. You were thirteen when Victoria pretended that her daughter committed suicide. Maybe that meant something to her, we'll never know. But what you did, you thought you were doing it for the girl you loved. In a way you still were. You stabbed Victoria, just like you stabbed Christine Morginson and Maeve Franklin. You were only thirteen, and because she had abused you, they sent you to a juvenile psychiatric facility until you turned eighteen, and then your records were sealed, you started over with a clean slate."

Started over, that was a joke.

He hadn't started over. He had barely been surviving each and every day since then.

Lavender was dead, and he had taken a life. In the hospital he had been treated like some sort of insane imbecile by the staff and his parents had been as disinterested in him as they had always been.

His life was hell.

It was nothing.

*He* felt like nothing.

Until Samara.

She was the first person ever, other than Lavender, to show him an ounce of kindness. To take time to make him feel like a real human being. She had cared enough to stop and find out if he was okay, and in doing so she had saved his life. Because of her, he hadn't jumped off the bridge and ended everything.

But now he knew the truth.

Lavender was nothing more than the imagination of an insane woman who had lost her mind after killing the daughter she had tortured.

Samara was all he had.

Sirens sounded in the distance, and the cops would be here soon. They would drag Samara away from him by force, shoot him if he resisted, throw him in prison for the rest of his life if he went with them peacefully.

Either way, the result would be the same.

He would be alone.

Again.

Without Samara.

He'd rather be dead.

Dante kept Samara close and jumped backward over the railing and off the bridge.

This was the only way they could be together.

Together in death.

Together for eternity.

No one was taking Samara away from him.

The fall seemed to last a lifetime.

Then with a splash, the icy river claimed them.

1:59 P.M.

Michael knew it was going to happen a split second before Dante jumped off the bridge taking Samara along with him.

The ground seemed to turn into quicksand.

He tried to get to Samara, but he couldn't move.

Instead, he was forced to watch everything play out in excruciatingly slow motion.

While Dante's face was full of peaceful conviction, Samara's was full of panic.

Her eyes met his.

They broadcast a mixture of terror, love, and resignation.

She believed that she was falling to her death.

As she toppled over and disappeared, he feared she was too.

Then like someone snapped their fingers, time sped up and he was running to the spot Samara had fallen. He reached it in time to see the splash as she and Dante hit the river.

"Don't."

Hands curled into his jacket and yanked him back.

"Get off me," he screamed.

"We'll drive down to the bottom of the hill and go into the river that way. To jump is suicide," Brady told him, trying to drag him away from the edge of the bridge.

"If we do that it'll take too long." If he jumped, he'd land approximately where Samara had. If they took the time to get back in the car, drive down, then swim out it would take so much longer. He'd have to search the water, and by the time he found her, it could be too late.

"It's suicide to jump," Brady said still trying to drag him away.

"I don't care." Without Samara what did he have to live for? A long slow self-inflicted death from killing his body with alcohol, that was it.

At least this would be quick.

Michael wrenched himself from his boss' grip and launched over the edge.

He didn't like heights, and he didn't like rollercoasters, and plummeting from the bridge to the river below felt like riding the world's highest rollercoaster.

He landed with a crash.

The cold momentarily stole his breath and then before he could properly fill his lungs with air he was under the water.

The force of the jump sent him down through the water, deeper and deeper until the light of the day disappeared, and all he was surrounded by was dark, cold water.

His lungs screamed for air, but instead of kicking his feet and trying to swim back up to the surface, he began to search.

She had to be here somewhere.

Only a minute, two at most, had passed since Dante tried to kill himself and Samara, and Samara was a good swimmer. He knew that because their gym had a pool they would sometimes swim laps instead of lifting weights and running on the treadmills, and she would outswim him every time.

She might have already made it to the shore.

Unless she'd been hurt when she hit the water. Falling from that height the landing could be like hitting concrete, especially since she probably would have landed awkwardly as Dante had been holding onto her.

Or he might have kept hold of her, dragged her down with him. His goal had been to kill himself and Samara because he couldn't face living without her, and he knew they weren't letting him walk away with her.

While Brady had driven, following the dot on the GPS that marked Samara's location, he had researched Dante Sundry. Because the woman whose house he had left Asher at had gotten his license plate they'd been able to find out who the car was registered to and everything they could about that person. They still didn't know how and where Dante had met Samara, but maybe once they found her, she'd be able to tell them.

His lungs were burning for oxygen, he couldn't stay under any longer.

Michael burst up through the surface and sucked in several gulps of air while he scanned the shoreline.

He couldn't see Samara anywhere.

She was still in the water, and if he didn't find her soon it was going to be too late.

He dove back down.

It was freezing, his muscles were aching, and he knew that he was going to become hypothermic sooner rather than later. Because it was so dull it was hard to see under the water, he swam back and forth, his head turning left and right, and left and right, looking for a large shape that could be Samara.

Michael was about to go back up to the surface to drag in another round of air before coming back down when he spotted something.

Two large shapes.

People-sized shapes.

Ignoring the need to breathe, he swam toward them.

It didn't take long, neither were moving, just kind of floating there, drifting slowly toward the bottom of the river.

The cold was almost paralyzing, his limbs were growing heavy, and his mind was growing numb. He wanted to lie down, close his eyes, go to sleep. He knew it was hypothermia clawing at him, lapping around him like the water, wanting to claim him. He fought against it. Samara needed him. He'd promised her that he wouldn't let the stalker hurt her and he had already failed once, he wasn't going to fail again.

Something like spider webs tangled around his hands.

Hair.

Samara's long dark hair fanned out around her, moving gently from side to side as it wafted with the water.

Michael grabbed hold of it and let it lead him to her body. As soon as he touched it, he curled an arm under her shoulders and kicked his feet.

He didn't get very far.

Something was pulling him back, pulling Samara and now him deeper into the river.

Keeping hold of Samara with one hand while his other ran up and down her body, he tried to find what was holding her down.

Dante.

His hand was locked around Samara's ankle.

Any second now his lungs were going to force him to take a breath, filling his lungs with ice cold water instead of air, and Samara had been in the water long enough that she hung limply in his arms.

With no time to spare, Michael willed his body to cooperate and slammed his boot into Dante's wrist.

That did the job.

The hand opened, and Dante floated away.

As fast as he could, Michael swam himself and Samara to the surface. He had to gulp in several mouthfuls of air before he could start swimming to the shore. His body was sluggish now, the cold was affecting him to the point that he wasn't even sure he could swim the fifteen yards or so to the edge of the river.

Then he saw lights, and cars, and Brady and Fin.

Help was here, he had to get Samara to it.

He hadn't saved his daughter.

He was going to save Samara.

Michael started to swim.

He didn't think of anything besides kicking his legs and pushing through the water with his spare arm.

"Here, I got her," Fin said when he reached the shore, and Michael reluctantly handed Samara over only because he wasn't sure he could stand and carry his own weight let alone hers as well.

Fin scooped Samara up and carried her to Brady's car, lying her out on the backseat.

"Is she okay?" he asked as Brady helped him pull himself out of the river and stagger to his feet.

"She's not breathing," Fin said, dragging her back out of the car and laying her down on the ground, beginning CPR.

Michael dropped to his knees beside Samara and grabbed her hand. He wanted to help Fin with the CPR, but he was still struggling to suck in enough air to keep his body working, let alone save Samara. Fin was a doctor, if anyone could save her it was him.

"Don't you dare die on me," he begged, squeezing her hand as tightly as he could. She was so cold, so still, it was like she was already gone. He felt like he was back in time eight years, clutching his daughter's lifeless body in his arms begging her to live.

That day his prayers hadn't been answered.

Was today going to have the same outcome?

Fin started the third round of CPR and Samara suddenly started to cough and splutter. Her brother rolled her onto her side while she coughed up the water that had nearly stolen her life. Before Michael could pull her into his arms, Fin had snatched her up and put her in the back of the car.

"Grab the blankets," Fin said to Brady.

While Fin stripped off Samara's soaked jeans and sweater, Michael dragged his numb body into the front seat. The heater was on, and although hot air blasted out, he was too wet and too cold for it to go any way toward warming him up. Fin took the blankets Brady handed him, wrapped Samara up in them, and pulled her into his lap.

She was shaking, her breath came in harsh gasps, but she was alive.

Then Michael heard the best sound in the world.

"Mike?"

"Right here, sweetheart." He reached between the seats to touch his hand to her cheek.

Samara lifted her head from her brother's shoulder to look at him. "You saved my life," she whispered, her voice rough and hoarse but still the most beautiful sound he had ever heard.

"It was nothing," he said and meant it. There wasn't anything he wouldn't do for her.

"Let me go." Samara squirmed in her brother's arms.

"You're hypothermic, and I just did CPR on you, an ambulance is coming, but you have to rest until it gets here," Fin told her.

"Michael. I need Mike," she protested.

"Fine," Fin relented. He picked her up, still swaddled in blankets, took her out of the car and around to the front, setting her on his lap.

"I love you," she whispered, snuggling against him and going limp as she passed out.

"I love you, too," he let his eyes close and just held her. Samara was alive, he hadn't lost her. Today God had answered his prayers.

# CHAPTER
## *Five*

December 24th
4:11 A.M.

He sat staring at the bottle.

Samara was safe, alive, sleeping in the hospital. Her stalker was dead, his body had been fished out of the river and was now at the morgue.

Michael should be feeling on top of the world.

But he wasn't.

Instead, he had been sitting in his kitchen for the last few hours, his elbows on his knees, staring at a bottle of whisky.

He wanted to drink it so badly.

Although he knew that Samara would be okay, his mind kept spinning with a litany of what-ifs.

What if he hadn't seen Samara in the water and been able to get her out in time for Fin to save her?

What if Brady had stopped him from jumping off the bridge, and by the time they drove down to the bottom of the river it was too late?

What if Dante had realized that Samara still had her phone on her and had thrown it away?

There were too many scenarios where things might not have turned out the way they had.

There were too many ways he could still lose Samara.

This was a time when he should be rejoicing that not only was Samara alive and safe now that her stalker was dead, but they were in love, and nothing was standing in the way of them starting their lives together.

Nothing except this bottle.

This bottle that he couldn't tear his eyes away from.

After Heidi's death, when he'd had to drink to dull the guilt enough to function, he'd worked a case much like the one Samara had just lived through. A young woman had been stalked by her ex, he'd been relentless, turning up at her house, vandalizing her car, following her to and from work. Stalking cases were always hard to prove and even harder to get a conviction, but then the guy had made it easy for them, he'd grabbed her at the supermarket parking lot one evening, tied her up, thrown her into the trunk of his car, and driven her back to the house they used to share.

The abduction had been reported, and he and his partner had been called.

It had been eight at night, and he was already drunk.

He'd written the address down wrong.

Written down fifty-three instead of thirty-five.

By the time they realized his mistake, it was too late.

Amy Mack was already dead.

That case had been the catalyst for him quitting his job and quitting drinking. He'd gone cold turkey thinking he was strong enough to resist the urge to drink ever again. He hadn't joined AA, he hadn't even let anyone know just how bad things had gotten with his drinking. His mistake in writing down the street number had been written off as just that—a mistake.

Just like his attitude to his drinking had been a mistake.

He hadn't taken ownership of his problem, he'd just brushed it aside, ascribed it to grief over Heidi's death, but that had been the coward's way out.

He was an alcoholic.

What more evidence did he need than the fact that instead of sitting in the hospital at the bedside of the woman he loved watching over her as she slept, he was sitting alone in his house at four in the morning contemplating throwing away seven years of sobriety just to erase—or even dull—the images of Samara going over the side of the bridge and splashing into water fifty feet below.

Michael picked up the bottle.

He held it in his hands, enjoying the feel of the smooth glass. Nothing else felt like it, not soda bottles or milk bottles. It was like the glass of a whisky bottle was possessed by what it held inside.

With a hand that was far too steady he unscrewed the lid.

Then he set the bottle down.

Stared at it once again.

He spun the bottle top between his fingers.

Round and around, then he tossed it across the room, it clinked as it hit the ground, and he heard it roll until it reached the wall and toppled down.

He should leave the bottle, go back to the hospital. Samara would wake up soon, and if he wasn't there she'd want to know why. The last thing Michael wanted was to add to her feelings of being abandoned. Enough people had walked out on her, and he didn't want her to think he was just another person to do it.

But he was, wasn't he?

He *wasn't* there.

He knew that she was going to need him and yet he wasn't there for her.

Michael picked up the bottle, held it to his lips, and tipped his head back. At the last second, he pressed his lips closed, the liquid splashed against them then dribbled down the sides of his chin.

With a sigh he set the bottle back down.

He felt trapped.

His need to drink was too strong, too powerful, sooner or later he was afraid that he would give into it, and he was even more afraid of what would happen when he did. What mistakes would he make when he was drunk? A mistake that would wind up hurting Samara?

It was like he was damned if he did and damned if he didn't.

If he left, he was hurting her, and yet if he stayed, he would wind up hurting her anyway.

Try as he might, he couldn't shake the feeling that if he just took a mouthful of the whisky that everything would be better. Just one mouthful. That was all he needed, surely one mouthful wasn't going to hurt.

Again, he picked up the bottle, held it, stared at it, longed to drink it.

Again, he lifted the bottle to his lips.

Just one mouthful.

Only one.

He'd stop after one.

His body burned for it like he was dehydrated and craving water.

But the whisky wasn't water, and his body didn't need it.

Michael threw the bottle against the wall, sending a shower of whisky and tiny glass shards raining down to the wooden floorboards.

Despite his satisfaction that he hadn't given in to the need to drink, he could barely contain the urge to get down on his hands and knees and lick up whatever liquid was there. He should have bought another bottle when he'd stopped off on the way back from the hospital.

This was never going to work.

He couldn't stay here.

Anxiety over every potential thing that could happen to Samara and how he would cope with it would destroy them both. He'd wind up drinking himself to death if he lost her, and possibly by having her as well.

Michael knew what he had to do.

He had to leave.

It would hurt Samara, but it would hurt less in the long run to do it now before either of them got any more attached than they already were. And it wasn't like he had much of a choice, his drinking would destroy them both if he let it, and he would never let anything hurt Samara.

Leaving the broken bottle on the floor, he headed to his bedroom, throwing a few clothes and his important papers into a suitcase. He picked up a framed photograph of him and Samara at her birthday party last spring. Just like she didn't really like Christmas, Samara wasn't a fan of birthday parties either, but he'd wanted to do something for her, so they'd thrown together a party complete with streamers and balloons, cake and ice cream, games and dancing, and dozens of presents.

Samara had laughed and smiled and enjoyed the night despite herself.

He wished he could go back to that day when everything had been fun and carefree.

Tossing the photo into the suitcase, he zipped it up, grabbed his keys, and headed out the front door.

Where he met Brady.

"What are you doing here? It's five o'clock in the morning. Shouldn't you be home with your pregnant wife?" Michael snapped. He'd made up his mind what he had to do, and he didn't want to risk anyone talking him out of it.

"You're bailing."

"I'm doing what has to be done."

"You're going to break her heart."

Michael locked his front door, walked past his friend, and climbed into his car. Reversing down the driveway he drove off into the early morning. Snow swirled around the car, houses were all dressed up for tomorrow, it was Christmas Eve, and while most were preparing to celebrate the holidays with their families, he was walking away from his chance to have everything he had ever wanted.

He'd driven nearly a mile before he said softly, "I'm saving her. Saving both of us."

～

2:36 P.M.


Something curled around her wrist.

Dante.

It was Dante dragging her to her death just because he wanted to die.

The cold water lapped at her, sealing over her head like the lid of a coffin slamming closed.

The shock of the icy water had stolen her breath.

She'd tried to swim back up toward the water, but Dante was there, pulling her down, his hand locked around her ankle, his weight too much for her to fight against.

Samara tried to fight against it now.

She kicked her legs and clawed with her hands.

Panic grew inside her.

She didn't want to die.

She and Michael had only just found each other. She didn't want to lose the chance at happiness she had thought she would never have.

"Samara. Samara."

Hands landed on her shoulders pressing her down as she tried to fight her way back to the surface.

She couldn't breathe.

The water was going to kill her.

"Samara, it's Fin. You're okay, you're just dreaming, you're in the hospital."

His words penetrated slowly, and her eyes popped open, still expecting to see gray water surrounding her in every direction.

"It's just the hospital," Fin said again.

Her vision cleared, the water faded, and in its place was the crisp white of the hospital room.

Her brother hovered above her, and she shrunk away from him.

Since Michael, Fin, and Brady had managed to track her and Dante down, she assumed that they had found Asher, but that didn't mean her brother had forgiven her.

She didn't want to see Fin right now, she wanted Michael. She scanned the room, but he wasn't there. Had something happened to him? Her memories were all fuzzy. She remembered being out in the cold, held tightly against Dante's chest as Brady attempted to talk him into giving himself up. She remembered Michael's eyes meeting hers, grounding her, giving her hope that everything would work out okay, keeping her from falling apart. Then she remembered falling, screaming, hitting the water, going under, then nothing ...

Obviously, she'd been rescued, but she didn't remember being pulled from the water or being brought here.

What if Dante had also been pulled from the water?

What if he'd hurt Michael?

What if he'd killed him?

Samara could feel her panic rising again.

She needed to see Michael, she needed to know that he was okay, that she hadn't lost him.

"It's okay," Fin said, releasing his grip on her shoulders and stepping back as though sensing she didn't want to see him right now.

If something had happened to Michael she would be completely alone in the world. Her brother hated her for what had happened to his son because of her, so she didn't foresee them having a relationship into the future. She didn't have any other family, so Michael was it for her.

"I'm sorry."

Confused, she looked at Fin. Was he talking to her? Why would he be saying sorry to her? He hadn't done anything. She was the one who had almost cost him his son.

"What?" she asked.

Fin ran his hands through his dark hair making it stand up on end. "You almost died because of me."

"Because of Dante," she corrected. Fin had nothing to do with that delusional man's behavior.

"No, because of me. You sacrificed yourself for Asher." Fin turned his back to her, but she could see his shoulders shaking.

This was it.

He was about to unleash his anger on her.

She would lie here and take it because what else could she do?

She deserved it.

She deserved every single thing he was going to say to her.

Samara steeled her shoulders and prepared herself for the onslaught she knew was coming.

"At the house yesterday, when the stalker called you to tell you where to go to trade yourself for Asher, I brushed you off, because of that, you just went to your stalker without any backup. If he had killed you, I never would have forgiven myself. I wasn't angry with you about your stalker, what he did wasn't your fault. Yesterday I was just scared. I'm sorry I took it out on you."

She didn't know what to say.

That was the last thing she had expected to hear from her brother.

"It's okay," she said. Of course he was scared, his two-year-old son was in danger, and she was the convenient target for his fear because it was her fault.

"No, it isn't okay." Fin spun around to face her again, his blue eyes a swirling mess of emotions. "I know."

Her heart stopped beating.

That was what it felt like anyway.

There was no way he could mean what she thought he meant.

No way.

She had only ever told two people.

Her psychiatrist in the hospital just after she'd attempted suicide, and Michael a couple of days ago.

There was no way her psychiatrist would have said anything, the woman had retired a couple of years ago, and she would have no reason to contact Fin. And she'd asked Michael not to tell anyone—especially her brother—and he had agreed.

So how did Fin know?

She must be wrong, he must be talking about something else.

"Samara, why didn't you tell me?" Fin came and sat on the edge of the bed beside her. He reached out a hand as though to hold hers but then stopped at the last second.

She just stared at him.

This was the last conversation she wanted to be having right now.

"All these years I thought that you tried to end your life because you couldn't deal with everyone walking out on us. I was angry at you because you wanted to leave me too, but if I'd known ..." he trailed off, jumped to his feet walked four steps, stopped, spun around to face her, opened his mouth to say something, then snapped it closed and walked back to the bed where he stood looking down at her.

Samara shrunk away from his gaze.

He knew.

Fin knew.

He knew that their grandfather had raped her for two years straight, which was why she had attempted suicide.

"Why didn't you tell me?" The anguish in her brother's voice was too much to bear. It was like no matter what she did, it was wrong, and someone wound up being hurt.

"I didn't want you to know," she mumbled, averting her gaze.

"Why?"

"Because I was scared and ashamed and I thought you wouldn't love me anymore if you knew, I thought you would leave me too. And then you were so angry with me after I tried to kill myself and I thought you would hate me even more if you knew the truth," she admitted, staring at the floor because she couldn't look at her brother's hurt face.

Fin sat back down on the bed and dragged her into his arms. "I'm sorry. I'm so sorry, Samara. I hate that you had to deal with that on your own. I hate that I made it worse by being angry with you when I had no right to be. I'm sorry that what I said to you yesterday made you think I didn't care if you were dead so long as Asher was okay. That is not true. I love my son, but I love you as well. I hate that you didn't know that."

"It's not your fault," she said automatically.

"Michael also said that your perfectionism thing is because you're trying to make up for what you did, stop doing that, you have nothing to make up for. Nothing," he said fiercely. "I love you, Sami."

"Really?"

"Always." He held her so tightly that she winced but wouldn't ask him to loosen his hold for anything.

Samara smiled despite the tears that were streaming down her cheeks. "Is Asher okay?"

"He's fine."

"What time is it?"

"Almost three in the afternoon. You slept for a long time, you were hypothermic, and there was some water in your lungs from the river."

"What about Asher's party?" she asked, pulling back. She didn't want her brother to miss his son's second birthday because he was here with her.

"We just changed it from lunch to dinner. You should be able to get out of here within an hour or two, enough time for you to come. If you're up to it."

She was up to it.

Nothing would make her miss her nephew's birthday, especially now that she and Fin had made up. She hadn't felt this close to her brother since she was nine years old.

"Where's Michael?" she asked. She was surprised that he wasn't here with her waiting for her to wake up, and she couldn't shake the feeling that something was wrong.

"Why don't you get a little more sleep and I'll go see about getting your discharge paperwork started," Fin said, taking hold of her shoulders and trying to lie her back down.

Samara shrugged off his hands, her panic amped up another notch. "Is he hurt? Did Dante do something to him?"

"No, he's not hurt, and Dante is dead, he won't ever hurt you again."

If Michael wasn't dead or injured, then where was he?

The gnawing ball of anxiety in her stomach grew. "Where is he?" she asked.

Fin sighed, and she didn't miss the anger that flashed through his eyes. "I'm sorry, Samara, he left."

"Left?" she echoed, unsure what that meant exactly.

"He's gone."

"Gone where?"

"I don't know. He left the hospital as soon as he was discharged. Brady went by his house early this morning, and Michael was leaving. With a suitcase."

A suitcase.

Michael had left with a suitcase.

She knew what that meant.

She had lived through it three times before.

He was gone.

And he wasn't coming back.

# CHAPTER

*Six*

December 25th
8:24 P.M.

"Are you sure you don't want to spend the night again?"

"I have to come home sooner or later," Samara reminded her brother as he pulled into her driveway.

"But it doesn't have to be today. Come and stay at our house again. You know Asher is going to be thrilled, and Chloe and I are happy to have you as long as you want to stay," Fin said.

She appreciated his offer.

She *really* did.

Fin had stayed with her in the hospital then driven her back to his place for Asher's party. Everyone had tried really hard to keep her busy and distracted, and while she appreciated their effort, it had just made her feel like everyone felt sorry for her because she'd nearly died and then instead of being there for her when she needed him, Michael had bailed.

Although she had slept nearly twenty-four hours straight in the hospital, she'd still been tired and had been pretty easily persuaded to spend the night.

Her brother and his family had happily included her in their Christmas morning fun of opening gifts, and then they'd gone to Sawyer and Ashley's wedding together. Her friend had looked stunning in her dress, and just as Ashley had wanted, it had been snowing. She was so happy for Ashley and Sawyer, but she couldn't deny that their wedding just served to remind her that she wasn't getting married. She was alone.

After that, it had been a joint Christmas dinner and wedding reception. Someone must have stopped by her house because all the gifts she had brought for everyone were under the tree at Ashley and Sawyer's house. Exchanging gifts and eating, with everyone laughing and talking should have been enough to distract her and keep her mind occupied, but it wasn't.

All she'd thought about was Michael.

It was like a piece of her was missing.

She physically felt the loss of his presence.

When he left, he'd left her with a hole in her heart she knew was never going to heal completely.

But now it was time to face the facts.

Michael was gone, and the sooner she came home and got used to that the sooner she could move on.

It was funny, Michael had only been staying at her house for a few days, but it had already started to feel like he had always been there.

She was really going to miss him.

"Thank you, your offer means a lot to me, but I have to do this," she told her brother.

Fin sighed. "Okay, but you know that I'm only a phone call away. If you need me, call me. Please, Samara, don't shut me out again, I *want* to be here for you."

Because of the pain and the sincerity in his voice she couldn't say no. "Okay. I'll call if I need anything."

"Good." Fin leaned over and kissed her cheek. "I'll stay until you're inside."

"Dante is dead now," she reminded him. "You don't need to worry about me anymore, I'm perfectly safe."

"I'll stay until you're inside," he repeated.

"Big brothers." She rolled her eyes.

"Little sisters," he shot back with a grin. "Try to get some more sleep, you've been through a lot in the last week, physically and emotionally. It's normal to be feeling tired, don't fight it."

Her brother the doctor, just couldn't help himself. "I'm going to go take a nice hot shower then go straight to bed," she promised. "And Brady already insisted that I take an extra week off from work, so I have plenty of time to recuperate." Samara dreaded the next two weeks where she would have nothing to do but sit around her house and think about Michael.

"You have painkillers and sleeping pills," Fin reminded her. "Use them if you need them. And remember, call if you need to. Even if you have nightmares and it's the middle of the night. Call, and I'll come."

"I will," she said then opened her door because Fin was just going to keep giving medical advice and reminding her to call if she needed anything until she got out of the car.

"Goodnight."

"Night."

With her brother's eyes watching her every move like a hawk, Samara walked to her front door, opened it, turned and waved, then stepped inside.

As soon as she did the pain of Michael leaving hit her right in the chest, piercing her heart.

Like a tap had been turned on her tears came in a flood, flowing down her cheeks and dripped down onto her clothes.

She leaned against the closed front door and slid down it till her bottom hit the floor, then she pulled her knees to her chest and sobbed without trying to fight against it.

Samara didn't know how long she sat there and cried, but by the time her tears finally dried up, she felt completely empty. She was tired but not sleepy, she hadn't eaten much today because she hadn't had much of an appetite, but now she was a little hungry. Maybe she'd have a piece of toast before she took a shower and went to bed.

Dragging herself to her feet, Samara headed for the kitchen but froze in the doorway.

The popcorn strings and paper chains she and Michael had made for Asher's party still lay on her kitchen counters. The Colorado Blue Spruce that they'd made into a little Christmas tree sat on the kitchen table. They'd never gotten around to making the star because they'd gotten the message about Hannah and the kids.

She had really thought that Michael was different.

She had believed that they had a future.

In just a couple of days, she had stopped seeing him as just her friend and started seeing him as the person that she could share her life with, and she had already been daydreaming about what it would be like.

And now just like that, without even giving her a chance to weigh in, it was over, and he was gone.

She'd been wrong.

Michael hadn't really been in love with her, he wasn't different, he was just the same as everyone else in her life. He saw her as a responsibility that he had to take care of and then once he'd done that he was done.

As bad as she felt right now, she would get through this.

It would leave a scar.

A big one.

But over time scars faded and hers would too.

Just like all her other scars had faded.

Maybe allowing herself to be vulnerable to Michael had helped her cross the barrier that had been holding her back, keeping her tethered to the past. She was finally ready to heal and move forward.

She wanted happiness, a family, a future.

As much as it hurt to look at the bonsai tree decorated as a little Christmas tree, she resisted the urge to take off the popcorn string and put the tree back outside with the others. She was going to leave it as it was, then every time she looked at it, she would remember what Michael had given her.

"You got this," she reminded herself aloud. "Let's make you a star, little Christmas tree."

Samara grabbed a roll of foil and a cardboard cereal box from the recycling, drew a star, and then cut it out. Once she'd wrapped the foil around it, she took it to the tree and set it on top. As much as she wished she was doing this with Michael, she was proud of herself for being able to do it on her own. Her whole life Christmas had been a symbol of the lack of family that she had, so standing here alone in her kitchen with her own Christmas tree was such a big step for her.

"You're stronger than you think you are." She would say it as many times as she needed to, as many times as it took to sink in, and one day she knew it would.

# CHAPTER
## *Seven*

One Year Later

December 24th
3:44 P.M.

Christmas Eve was here again.

It was like she had blinked and the last year had passed.

It was hard to believe that this time last year she had woken up in the hospital thinking that she and Michael had their whole lives to spend together only to learn that he had left.

She hadn't heard from him since.

Samara sighed and lay down on her bed.

Another Christmas.

Another Christmas *alone*.

Over the last twelve months, Samara had changed a lot. She'd strengthened her relationships with her family and her friends. She worked even harder at her job, she'd even started a charity to support other victims of stalking. She had also jumped into the dating scene. So far none of them had turned into anything serious, but it felt good to finally move forward.

Now that Christmas was back though, she couldn't stop thoughts of Michael from invading her mind. Part of her still wanted him, which was stupid, he had made it abundantly clear that a relationship with her wasn't what he wanted.

Still, she couldn't forget him no matter how hard she tried.

He was her first love, and even though they had only spent such a short time together as a couple, the mark he had left on her heart was a deep one.

The doorbell rang.

She wanted to ignore it, but it was Christmas Eve, and she didn't know why anyone would be knocking on her door unless it was important.

Had she missed a phone call or text?

She rolled over and picked up her phone from the nightstand, but there were no missed calls or messages waiting for her. Maybe it was a neighbor who needed help with something.

Smothering a yawn with her hand, Samara headed downstairs and threw open the front door, and the words she had been about to say froze on her lips.

It was Michael.

*Michael.*

Standing on her doorstep.

For a moment she thought she must be hallucinating and rubbed at her eyes, but he didn't disappear.

She didn't say anything, and neither did he.

If she had to guess they stood there in silence, staring at each other for a full five minutes before she finally snapped to her senses.

Samara had the door half-closed before Michael suddenly shot out an arm and stopped her.

"I missed you," he said. The pain and anguish in his voice said that he had, but he was the one who had left and stayed away. If he had wanted to see her there had been nothing stopping him.

She didn't know what to say to that, so she just tried to push the door closed.

But Michael had his hand on it, and he wasn't budging.

If he wasn't going to let her shut the door, then she'd just leave it open and walk away. If Michael could walk away, then she saw no reason why she couldn't do it as well.

She hadn't gone more than two steps toward the stairs when Michael's hand wrapped around her wrist, holding her in place.

The second he touched her all those feelings that she had been attempting to bottle up for twelve months came flooding back. The strength of them almost knocked her off her feet.

Why did he have to come back?

She had been working so hard to let go and move on, and now he was ruining that.

It was too late for them.

Wasn't it?

Samara mentally berated herself. Why was she thinking of picking up where things had left off when Michael had abandoned her, and she didn't even know why he was here?

"I'm sorry," he said, his voice agonized. "I'm so sorry I hurt you."

She wanted to press her lips into a line and refuse to be engaged in conversation, but she wasn't going to sulk. If there was one thing the last twelve months had taught her it was that she had spent enough time in the dark. Now she was determined to seek the light every day. "Why did you leave?"

"I'm an alcoholic, Samara. When I jumped off that bridge after you and found you in the water in time to save your life, I should have been happy, relieved that it was over, that you were safe. Of course, I was relieved that you were okay, I don't know what I'd do if anything happened to you, but all I could think about was what I would have done if you'd died. I couldn't function. I sat in my kitchen for hours staring at a bottle of whisky. I couldn't start something with you while I was in that place. That wouldn't have been fair to you or to me. So, the last year I went to rehab, I joined AA, I have a sponsor, I have a therapist, and I'm working through my feelings about Heidi's death. I love you and if I was going to have any shot at a life with you, then I have to have it together, otherwise I'm going to wind up hurting you, or me, or both of us. I didn't have my drinking under control then, but I do now."

"I'm happy for you," she said. And she meant it. She didn't want Michael to let alcohol destroy him.

"Walking away was the hardest thing I ever had to do," he continued. "I wouldn't have done it if I didn't love you. I would have just kept walking the tightrope I'd been balancing on since Heidi died, pretending I was okay. But I'm here now, and I want you back, so the only question is, did I ruin things by walking away?"

Her heart said no, but her head said yes.

She had taken such a leap of faith by letting herself fall for him, and he'd left. Even if he'd had a good reason he had still walked away, and she didn't know if she could trust that he wouldn't do it again.

"Thank you for taking the time to tell me all of this, I truly am glad that you took the time to work on yourself." Her tone was a little dismissive, but she was doing the best she could.

"Let me take you out to dinner."

"It's Christmas Eve." It was a lame excuse and she knew it.

"And you hate being alone at Christmas, so let me make sure that you're not. Please, just dinner, the two of us, if nothing else, it will take your mind off the holidays."

It would be so simple to say yes.

She wanted to pick back up where they had left off, but she didn't know what the right thing to do was.

"You kept the Christmas tree," Michael said. Releasing her wrist, he walked across the room to a small table in a corner of the living room where the Colorado Blue Spruce Christmas tree sat, decorated just as it had been last Christmas.

"I couldn't get rid of it."

Her eyes followed him as he walked over to the tree and picked it up. He looked so good. The same as he had the last time she'd seen him and yet different somehow. He looked less stressed, more at peace, the guilt was gone from his eyes and his stance. It was like a weight had been lifted off his shoulders. That reassured her a little. He was here now because he wanted to be, he had his life sorted out, and now he had come to see if they could sort things out as well.

"Dinner?" Michael asked, appearing before her. He picked up her hand and lifted it to his mouth, pressing a kiss to her palm and then the inside of her wrist.

Samara shivered.

How could one pair of lips make her feel so good?

How could they erase twelve months of pain, and doubt, and loneliness?

"Will you let me spend Christmas Eve with you and take you to dinner?"

4:15 P.M.

He waited anxiously for Samara's answer.

Had he waited too long to return?

This past year had been the longest of Michael's life. He'd worked as hard as he could to get himself together so he could come back for Samara. Every day he had wanted to call her, tell her he was sorry for leaving like he had, and tell her why it was so important that he sort himself out before they could start their lives together.

Assuming she still wanted a life with him.

Every day he had worried that leaving the way he had caused irreparable damage to their relationship, but he hadn't known any other way to do it. If he'd gone to see her in the hospital, he wouldn't have been able to leave, and that would have left him balancing precariously between sobriety and an alcohol-fueled downward spiral. Sooner or later, life would have thrown something difficult at them, and he would have turned back to the bottle.

But now for the first time since he'd turned to alcohol to numb the pain of killing his daughter, he felt like he had a handle on his drinking. He was always going to be an alcoholic, and there was always the chance that he might fall off the wagon, but he had given himself the best chance he could of remaining sober.

Because he had noticed the way it affected her, Michael pressed another light kiss to the inside of Samara's wrist and was satisfied to see her shiver in response. Was it fair to try to manipulate her like that? Maybe not, but he was here to win her back, and he knew he stood a chance because she'd kept the decorations on the little bonsai Christmas tree they'd made last year.

"I guess," Samara said a little uncertainly, but he'd take it.

"Thank you for giving me another chance." Michael dipped his head to kiss her, then thought better of it, she wasn't in that place yet, so instead he touched his lips to her forehead. "You are so much more than I deserve."

She fought the urge to disagree with him, he could see it in her big, beautiful blue eyes, but instead she asked, "I'm still dressed in what I wore for Asher's party, is this okay or should I change? I don't know where we're going for dinner."

While she looked stunning in a simple ankle-length denim skirt, black boots, and purple sweater that nicely complemented her pale skin, dark hair, and bright blue eyes, she'd be too cold for what he had planned. "Go change into something warm," he said. "And don't forget your coat, scarf, mittens, and beanie."

Samara looked curious now. "Where are we going?"

"All in good time." He winked. It had been so long since he'd felt playful and relaxed like this. Carrying around his guilt over his daughter's death had changed him, but he was learning how to be the man he'd been before.

She arched a brow but didn't ask any more questions and gently tugged her hand from his grip to hurry up the stairs. She returned a few minutes later in jeans, fur-lined boots, a green turtleneck sweater, with the required coat, scarf, mittens, and beanie in her arms.

"Let's go." Michael grinned, he knew he would have to work to earn Samara's trust back, but he thought he had a pretty good first step planned out.

Although he wanted to hold her hand, he didn't want to push too hard too soon, so they walked side by side down the driveway to his car. He opened the door for her and closed it once she'd buckled her seatbelt. The drive was mostly silent, he was nervous about whether he could ever make up for hurting Samara, and she was no doubt wondering if she should or shouldn't give him a second chance.

"We're here," he announced as he parked the car.

"The park?" Samara sounded confused. "You want to have a picnic? There's a foot of snow on the ground and more coming down."

"I remember the first time Heidi saw snow. She was eleven months old and just learning to walk. It was my week to have her, and we were coming back from the grocery store. I took her out of her car seat and put her down in the front yard while I grabbed the bags and snowflakes started to fall. She was so excited, she didn't know what to make of it. She kept toddling about everywhere, as fast as her little legs would carry her, trying to catch the snowflakes on her hands." He smiled at the memory. It was getting easier to think about the good times with his daughter without feeling like the world was going to open up and swallow him whole.

"I bet she looked so cute." Samara reached out and laid a hand on top of his.

"She did. You look kind of cute yourself." He smiled.

Samara made a face at him, and put on her coat, scarf, mittens, and beanie, and climbed out of the car. "Is the picnic basket in the trunk? Do you need help carrying everything?"

"Nope."

"Are we going to walk to a restaurant to get dinner then?"

"Nope."

"So, what are we eating?"

"You'll see." This time he took her hand and began to lead her through the park, past the playground, around the lake to a small gazebo on the other side.

"Oh, Mike." Samara gasped when she saw it. "It's beautiful."

He'd had fairy lights strung up around the whole thing, and it glowed and sparkled in the quickly approaching dark. "Not as beautiful as you."

She looked up at him and her cheeks pinked. "You were pretty confident I'd say yes to the date."

Michael shook his head. "Not confident, just hopeful. Come on, there's more." He pulled her on and was rewarded with another gasp as they walked up the three steps and into the gazebo. There was a small fire in a wood-burning camp stove at the far end of the gazebo, in the center was a round table set for a candlelight dinner for two, and dozens of rose petals scattered across the floor. With all the fairy lights the place had a magical feel that he hoped Samara could feel as well.

"It's gorgeous," Samara gushed. "I've never been on a date like this before."

He knew that she had dated a little over the last year, he'd been keeping tabs on her through Brady, and while he hated the thought of her with another man, he was glad that she finally saw that she deserved to have a happy future. "We have music too," he told her, pressing an app on his cell phone that was linked to the speakers he'd set up earlier. An original recording of Winter Wonderland sung by Richard Himber filled the gazebo.

"That song is perfect." He still held Samara's hand, and she squeezed his tightly. "Thank you for doing all of this for me."

"Thank you for agreeing to come." Samara stared up at him, and he stared down at her, their eyes locked together like magnets. Her lips parted just the tiniest bit, and Michael was just dipping his head when the sound of bells jingled in the air.

"What's that?" Samara asked, her eyes excited as she looked about.

"Sleigh bells," he replied. "Just like in the song. I thought we might take a little ride before dinner." Hand in hand, he led her out of the gazebo and around to the back of it where a sleigh pulled by a single horse wearing bells stood waiting for them.

"You really thought of everything." Samara clapped her hands delightedly.

It had taken a fair bit of effort to pull all of this off. Arranging the horse and sleigh, getting permission to have them here in the park, setting up the gazebo, having someone here to serve the meal, but it was all worth it to see the smile on Samara's face. "I just wanted tonight to be special for you. From now on, when you think of Christmas, I want you to think of this. Of how magical everything was, the snow, and the sleigh, the music, the lights, even if we don't end up together." Michael was very aware that his decision to leave might make that a reality. "I don't want you to think of Christmas time as a time when you're alone and sad. I want you to think of this and remember that there is always one person in the world who loves you more than anything else."

"Thank you," she said. The words were simple, but the emotion in them told him that she would. From now on she *would* think of this when she thought about Christmas time. Even if they didn't end up together, he could take solace in the fact that he had brightened the dark days in her life.

"Ready to go for a ride?"

"Dying to."

He held out his hand to help her into the sleigh, and she smiled at him as she took it and climbed in. Michael joined her, spread a blanket over their knees, and took the reins. The clip-clop of the horse's hooves and the sound of tinkling bells filled the evening. With the snow swirling around them it really was magical. The only thing that would make things perfect was Samara telling him that she forgave him and they could work things out.

*Be patient*, he reminded himself.

She still had at least some feelings for him. In time he believed he could repair the damage he had caused.

"When do I get to drive?" Samara asked.

Michael laughed.

Love was crazy and unpredictable and sometimes painful, but then it gave you moments like this one. Moments where even the pain and heartache were worthwhile just to experience one beautiful, perfect second with the person you loved.

Moments like this you cherished with every fiber of your being.

8:38 P.M.

This had been one of the best nights of her life.

Michael had really gone all out to make this night special. The dinner in the gazebo had been amazing, with the snow falling and the fire crackling and the music playing, and all the lights, it had been magical. And the sleigh ride had been the icing on the cake. It had been an incredible night, and she didn't want it to end.

But it had.

They were driving back to her house now, and then they'd say goodbye, and she'd go to bed alone.

Or would she?

Samara was so confused.

She still didn't know what to do about Michael.

He wanted the two of them to get back together, that's what tonight had been all about. She still loved him, she knew he knew that, but she wasn't sure about them being a couple. Perhaps they should just go back to being friends. That way he could always be a part of her life, but she didn't have to think about risking her heart again.

"Hey," Samara said as they approached her house. "What's with my house?"

"Just another little surprise," Michael replied, sounding both excited and a little smug.

"*Little* surprise?" she repeated. Lights were strung all around her roof. On her lawn was an illuminated Santa in a sleigh and four reindeer, and as they pulled into the driveway she could see a large green wreath with silver and gold baubles hanging on her front door.

"You like it?"

"I love it. Who did you get to do this while we were having dinner?"

"You'll see when we get inside."

She assumed he'd managed to wrangle a couple of their friends and ask them to help out with another surprise for her. She didn't know who since her brother Fin and Chloe had three-year-old Asher and were a month away from having their second child. Tom and Hannah had two little girls now, three-year-old Noelle and seven-month-old Joy. Brady and Aurora had nine-month-old Star, and Sawyer and Ashley had two-month-old twins Jackson and Janelle. She couldn't imagine that any of them would have the time to come and decorate her house, they'd want to be spending time with their families on Christmas Eve.

When they stepped inside her house, she realized exactly what Michael had done.

Garlands strung with lights circled the banisters, the doorways, and the fireplace mantle. A stocking hung by the fireplace, a huge Christmas tree was in the corner, decorated with lights, tinsel, and dozens of decorations. Under the tree were boxes of gifts wrapped in brightly colored paper. She could smell the cookies and gingerbread even before she saw the plates on the coffee table, everything looked delicious, and the gingerbread house looked amazing. On a small table by the tree, there was a plate with a couple of cookies, a bunch of carrots, a glass of milk, and a copy of 'Twas the Night Before Christmas. A sprig of mistletoe hung above the front door.

This was everything she had told Michael when he'd asked her what her perfect Christmas had looked like.

He hadn't forgotten a single thing.

This was the nicest thing anyone had ever done for her.

Everyone was there: her brother and his family, her friends, her bosses and their extended families. He must have rallied everyone to come and work together so that it would all be finished by the time he brought her home.

And he'd done it for her.

Samara was so grateful, she wanted to thank everyone, but tears were burning the backs of her eyes, she was so overwhelmed. Her mouth couldn't form all the words in her heart and embarrassed to cry in front of all these people she turned and ran up the stairs.

In her bedroom, she flung herself down on the bed and let her tears flow.

Why did Michael have to go and be so sweet?

It made deciding what she should do so much harder.

"Hey." A gentle hand rested on her shoulder. "You okay?"

"I'm sorry," she cried, burying her face in her pillow.

"About what?" The bed dipped as Michael sat beside her.

"I was going to turn you down, tell you that we couldn't be a couple and that we should just stay friends, even after that wonderful date you just took me on because no one has ever broken my heart like you did. But then we get back here, and you did all of this for me, you remembered every single thing that I said a year ago, and you took it and made it a reality, and now I feel so bad."

"Samara," he said, his tone full of tender affection. He took hold of her shoulders and sat her up, pulling her sideways so she sat in his lap. "Don't be sorry. If you want to turn me down, you can, I understand. I shouldn't have stayed away for so long. At first, I didn't realize it would take me a year to get myself together, I thought I'd be gone for a month, maybe two or three tops, not twelve. I'm so sorry that I let so much time pass before coming back, that was a mistake. I guess I was scared that I had already lost you, and coming back and getting confirmation of that was terrifying. I wanted to call you every day. I wanted to tell you how proud I was of you for finding the strength to move on and tell you that you don't ever have to be perfect with me. I don't want you to put that kind of pressure on yourself, I just want real. I just want you. I wanted to tell you what I was doing and why. I love you so much that I couldn't let my problem end up bringing you down."

"You didn't even give me a chance to offer to be there for you, to help you."

"You're right, I didn't. I'm sorry. It just didn't seem fair to ask you to."

"It's up to me to decide what's fair for me and what's not."

"I know, but I wasn't sure I could do it. I wasn't sure I could ever be in a place where I felt confident that I had my drinking under control. I'm always going to be an alcoholic, and that urge to drink is always going to be there, especially when things are tough, but I have the best motivation in the world to stay sober."

"Oh yeah?" She smiled through her tears.

"Yeah." He leaned in as though to kiss her but paused millimeters from her lips. His eyes met hers, seeking permission, and when she nodded, he kissed her. As he did the last of her doubts melted away. It hurt her that he hadn't given her the chance to help him and that he'd left the way he had and stayed away so long, but when it boiled down to it, she had two options; she could turn him down, insist they only be friends and be miserable, or she could accept that everyone makes mistakes and take him back and be happy.

When she looked at it like that there was only one choice.

"You kept tabs on me, didn't you?" Samara asked. It was the only way he could have known that she was working to move on.

"Brady, but don't be mad."

"I'm not mad," she assured him. "You worked on your drinking, I worked on my need to try to be perfect. Maybe last Christmas just wasn't the right time for us. But now ..." she snuggled closer and breathed in the scent she had missed for twelve long months, "now is the time for a fresh start."

"I love you so much." Michael kissed her neck, then her jaw, and then her lips. The kiss started soft and sweet but quickly morphed into something more passionate, more desperate. Michael's hands moved to the hem of her sweater, and his fingertips began to trace their way up her stomach to her breasts.

As much as she wanted this they couldn't, not now, not while everyone was downstairs waiting for them. "We can't," Samara said, breaking the kiss and pushing Michael's hands away. "We have guests."

"They can wait."

"No, they can't." She laughed. "Weren't you the one calling me impatient last Christmas?"

"Okay," he reluctantly agreed, pouting like a sulking child, and she laughed again.

They might have realized they were in love last Christmas, but in hindsight, neither of them had been ready for a serious relationship. They had both needed to work on themselves first. But now they were both in the right place at the right time. This Christmas they could start their lives together.

"When everyone leaves I'm going to ravish every inch of your delectable body until you forget the names of every single person who ever hurt you. I'm going to give you the merriest Christmas of your life. Of anyone's life," Michael told her.

She shivered. The good kind. A shiver of excited anticipation.

"One more kiss before we go down?" Michael held up the mistletoe that had been hanging above her front door.

How could she say no to that?

# CHAPTER
## *Eight*

December 25th
12:19 A.M.

"Okay, I got another one," Brady announced.

Everyone groaned.

Brady had been reading out lame Christmas jokes from his phone for the last hour, each one cheesier and cornier than the last.

"How is the alphabet on Christmas Day different than every other day?" Brady asked.

They all looked around, none of them sure of the answer.

"Anyone?" Brady asked. "No? Okay, on Christmas Day it has Noel."

Samara laughed.

Michael couldn't get enough of hearing that.

They sat side by side on the couch, holding hands, she was pressed right up against him as her brother and Chloe sat on her other side. They'd all been laughing, and playing charades, and reminiscing about past Christmases. The kids were all asleep, and it was after midnight. As much as he wanted to have Samara all to himself—preferably naked and upstairs in bed—he was enjoying seeing her having fun like this.

It seemed like they had both grown a lot in the last twelve months. Maybe his decision to leave had ended up working out for the best. As much as he hated that he'd hurt Samara, he knew they were both now in the right place to begin a relationship. Although begin seemed too strong a word, they'd been friends for years, he'd been in love with her for years, she'd loved him for the last twelve months, it felt like they had been together for years rather than just beginning their lives as a couple.

"We better get going," Sawyer announced. "The twins are going to need feeding again soon, and we have a big day tomorrow."

"You're on tomorrow, Sis," Fin said to Samara as he stood up. "We'll all be back here in twelve hours."

"I can't wait," Samara said, her eyes sparkling with glee. The last thing Samara had mentioned when they'd discussed her perfect Christmas last year was everyone gathered at her house celebrating Christmas lunch together.

"We'll bring the food," Brady said, "you just need to try to find places for all of us to sit."

That was going to be no easy feat.

It wasn't just Samara's family coming, but Brady and Aurora and their kids, Sawyer and Ashley and their kids, Sawyer's sister Savannah and her family, Tom and Hannah and their kids, and their other bosses Paige Hood and her family, and Ryan and his entire extended family. There was going to be over fifty people here at lunchtime tomorrow.

Samara laughed again. "As long as some of us don't mind sitting on the floor I think we can manage."

They exchanged hugs and kisses and Merry Christmases, and then everyone piled out into the snowy night.

Then they were alone.

Michael slipped his arms around Samara's waist and drew her up against him. "I've been waiting all night to have you to myself."

"I can never thank you enough for all of this." Samara rested her hands on his chest and stood on her tiptoes to kiss his cheek. "It was amazing. It was everything I ever longed for when I was a little girl. I'm never going to forget tonight. Ever. It was perfect. Just perfect. And just sitting around with everyone, talking and laughing and playing games, I think that was my favorite part."

"Oh?" He nibbled on her earlobe. "Your favorite part? I thought the best part of the night was still to come."

She giggled but pushed him away. "We have to clean up, and then we have to be up early tomorrow to get everything ready, so we should probably—"

He cut her off with a kiss. "Don't finish that sentence," he warned. "The mess can wait until the morning, and between the two of us, it won't take long to get everything ready. Besides, we can sleep tomorrow night, tonight is about us, and I don't want to do anything but make love to you over and over again."

"How can I say no to that?" Samara threaded her fingers in his hair and kissed him.

There was so much more to the kiss than just a kiss. It was full of emotion, hope for the future, safety and security, but also passion, and most importantly love.

Michael scooped her up, intending to carry her up the stairs, but she stopped him. "Let's stay down here. The tree, and the garlands, and all the lights, it's so pretty and magical."

"That we can do, I'll grab a blanket." He set her down in front of the tree and ran to the linen closet to get a blanket to lay out on the floor.

When he returned to the living room, he found Samara holding the bonsai tree they'd decorated last year. He'd told the others to make sure they left it out when they were decorating the house, but now that she had a real tree and her dislike of Christmas had been turned around they probably didn't need it anymore.

"Want me to take that back outside with the others?" he asked.

"No," she said quickly, holding the tree tightly. "I want to keep it just like this forever. Last Christmas when we decorated this it was the first time I ever enjoyed anything Christmassy. After you left, I thought about taking the popcorn strings off, but I couldn't, it was a symbol for me, of moving on, of trying to let the past stay in the past. I think I'm still going to need that reminder some days. Every time I look at this cute little tree, I'll think about you and how you turned my life around."

"You did the same for me," he told her. "After Heidi, part of me wished I was dead too, but now I don't. Now I want to have a future with you, maybe have more kids in the future, if you want to," he added quickly. They hadn't discussed the prospect of having children, so he wasn't sure exactly where Samara stood on the subject.

"Oh, I want to. I'd love to have a big family, at least three or four kids," Samara said, and from the look in her eyes, he knew she wanted to make up for everything she had missed out on.

"I think I can manage that." Michael took the bonsai tree from her arms and set it back down beside the big tree, then he picked Samara up and laid her down on top of the blanket he'd spread out in front of the fireplace. With the crackling fire in front of them, the Christmas tree beside them, all the fairy lights twinkling, he couldn't think of a more perfect place to make love for the first time officially a couple.

His eyes met Samara's, and the love shining through them hit him right in the heart. He'd never had a woman look at him like that before. His daughter had loved him but that was different, that was the love of a father and child, he'd never been *in* love before.

This feeling inside him right now was indescribable.

It filled him up, every single atom of his being touched by it.

It was almost like it was alive.

Michael couldn't imagine doing anything to ruin this.

He knew he would never do anything to shatter her trust in him ever again.

He didn't break eye contact as he leaned down and kissed her. Even when her eyes fluttered closed, he didn't look away. He wanted to watch every reaction. He wanted to see the emotions and feelings fly across her face, he wanted to memorize every single second of this.

"Condom?" he asked.

"We don't need one. I want to feel every inch of you, and I don't care if we make a baby."

Neither did he.

His hands found their way to her stomach and slipped under her sweater. Her skin was so soft, so smooth, he could touch her forever and never get enough. While one hand drifted higher, claiming one of her breasts and kneading it, the other dipped lower inside her waistband to touch her in the place he couldn't wait to be buried inside.

"Michael," she moaned, squirming restlessly beneath him.

"Impatient as ever, I see," he teased, continuing to drive her crazy with his hands, applying just enough pressure to make her wild but not enough to let her come.

"Please," she whimpered.

That was enough to snap the string binding his self-control, and he eased her jeans and panties down her legs, then shoved off his own and pushed inside her in one smooth thrust.

~

1:02 A.M.

Finally.

Finally, Michael was inside her.

Samara didn't think she would have been able to wait another second. She had *needed* him, she'd needed to feel close to him, needed their bodies to be joined together so that she knew that what she was feeling was real and not just excitement and joy over the amazing evening he'd given her.

But as they moved together, she knew.

For sure.

Without a single ounce of a doubt.

She loved Michael. Together they could have everything.

The happy future with a family of her own that she had always dreamed about. By this time next year, they might be married, maybe even have a baby on the way.

Michael moved faster, and Samara felt that feeling building up in her stomach. She matched his speed, her fingers tangling in his hair as she brought his mouth down to hers. One of his hands slipped between them, circling her hard little bundle of nerves with the pad of his thumb.

A minute later the world exploded into a million little brightly colored twinkling fairy lights.

They were both panting and breathless, and Michael pulled out then wrapped his arm around her, rolling them both over so the blanket was tucked around them and she was closer to the fireplace.

She could stay like this forever.

Lying in the arms of the man she loved, the crackle of the flames, the glow of the lights, this feeling in her heart, she wanted to freeze time so this moment never had to end.

"I love you, Mike," she whispered, nuzzling his neck.

"Right back at you," he murmured, tugging on a lock of her hair. "I have something for you."

"Hmm?" She was only half-listening, still blissfully locked in the moment, glad Michael had decided they should do this instead of cleaning up.

"You're not listening," Michael said, playfully poking her in the ribs.

"You expect me to concentrate after that?" She poked him back.

"I *was* pretty amazing." The smile he gave her was smug.

"*We* were," she corrected with a giggle. She liked this relaxed, fun side of Michael. She liked this relaxed, fun side of herself, too. "What did you say?"

"I have a Christmas gift for you."

"Aren't we supposed to wait for Christmas morning to exchange gifts?"

"It *is* Christmas morning," he reminded her. He sat them up and reached over to grab a red and green striped bag from under the tree. He reached inside and pulled out a small gold box and gave it to her.

"Thank you," she said as she took it and tore the paper. Inside was a bottle of hydrangea perfume. "Oh, pretty," she gushed, taking it out of its box. "I love hydrangeas, they come in such beautiful colors."

"I chose it because I knew that the association with Dante and your old perfume would mean you stopped wearing it.

"How did you know that?" she asked. He was right, but that wasn't information he would have been able to get from Brady. She hadn't told anyone about throwing out the lavender perfume after she got home last Christmas Day and never buying another bottle.

He smiled and brushed the back of his knuckles across her cheek. "Because I know you. I know how your mind works. I chose the hydrangea on purpose because they mean heartfelt and honest emotions, gratitude and thanksgiving, a deep understanding between two people, asking for forgiveness, and expressing regret. I thought that was perfect for us. We understood each other in a way no one else ever had. You're the first woman I've ever felt true emotion for. I'm so grateful for you being in my life—you *gave* me my life back. And after how I behaved this last year, I'm definitely regretful over hurting you and needing your forgiveness."

Tears welled up in her eyes. She had really lucked out with Michael. It made all the years she had been alone worth it because without them the path her life had taken would never have led her to him.

"I never got a chance to thank you for what you did that day," Samara said. "Fin told me how you jumped off the bridge after us with no thoughts for your own safety. How you wouldn't leave the freezing cold river until you found me. You saved my life. Thank you." The words didn't feel like enough even if she meant them more than she had ever meant anything in her life.

"There isn't anything I wouldn't do for you, you know that, right?" Michael pressed his thumb to her cheek to catch the tears that were falling and brushed them away.

"I know," she assured him.

"Good, because I have one more thing in here, you might say that it's too soon, but I don't believe it is."

Samara gasped.

He wasn't really going to do what she thought he was going to do, was he?

"Michael," she cautioned.

He ignored her and pulled out a small velvet box. He loosened the blanket that was wrapped around them and climbed out of it. Kneeling beside her, he reached for her hand.

"Samara, I love you. I know that I want to spend the rest of my life with you. We've been friends for years, and that friendship grew into something I thought I could only ever dream about. But you're real. You're sweet, and smart, and compassionate. I want to have kids with you, I want to grow old with you and spend every day of the rest of my life making up for all the bad things that have happened to you. Will you marry me?"

She drew in a breath.

Her heart wanted to say yes, but her brain wanted to say it was too soon. They should date for a while first, make sure that they are compatible as a couple and not just as friends.

But this time last year she had taken a leap of faith when she'd realized that she had feelings for Michael and decided to do something about it. And when Michael had left, she had promised herself that she would live for the future from that day forward.

All her life she had dreamed about someone like Michael, someone who loved her, someone who thought she was special, someone she could trust.

She knew he was all those things.

"Okay," she said with a shaky nod.

"Okay?" Michael echoed like he hardly dared to believe it.

"Okay," she repeated, calmer this time, whether it was too soon or not this was the right decision for them.

"Okay." Michael wrapped an arm around her waist and lifted her feet off the floor, spinning them both around and around the room until she was dizzy. Finally, he set her down on her feet and dropped to his knees again, taking her left hand and sliding the ring onto her finger. "I bought this Christmas Day last year, on my way to rehab. I've prayed every day since that when I gave it to you, you would say yes, that you could forgive me for walking out on you like so many other people had."

Samara dropped to her knees and cupped his cheeks in her hands. "I could never be angry with you for wanting to get your drinking under control. Do I wish you had given me the chance to help you on your journey? Yes. But last Christmas I promised myself that the past was staying in the past. And it is. You and I, we're the future. The past will always be there, I won't ever forget what happened to me, and I don't want you ever to forget your little girl, we'll celebrate Heidi every day, but if two people ever deserved some happiness, I think it's us."

"We've done the bad in life. From here on out it's going to be all sunshine and rainbows and unicorns."

"Unicorns, huh?"

"It could be." He laughed. "If we have a little girl this place will no doubt be brimming with unicorn stuff."

She laughed too. That sounded so perfect. Little boy or little girl, she didn't care what she and Michael had. She just wanted to have something that was half her and half him, someone who was a living, breathing symbol of their love.

"I love you so much," she told Michael. She'd already told him that, but she loved the way the words sound and couldn't get enough of saying them.

"I love you, too."

Samara kissed him, and since they were both still naked, she reached down to curl a hand around him. He responded instantly.

"Ready to go again, huh? Bet you're glad I said we should leave the cleaning up until later," he said smugly.

"You don't have to brag." She giggled, squeezing him and feeling a little smug herself at the subsequent groan that tumbled from his lips.

"Merry Christmas, Samara," Michael said as he laid her down and balanced his weight on his elbows above her.

"It really is. For the first time ever, it *is* a merry Christmas, and that's all because of you."

Making love to her fiancé in the early hours of Christmas morning, what could be a better way to celebrate her newfound love of Christmas, and the start of the rest of their lives?

**Can danger could spark something between these childhood friends? Find out in the next book in this thrilling romantic suspense series!**

Yuletide Hero (Christmas Romantic Suspense #6)

# Also by Jane Blythe

Detective Parker Bell Series

A SECRET TO THE GRAVE

WINTER WONDERLAND

DEAD OR ALIVE

LITTLE GIRL LOST

FORGOTTEN

Count to Ten Series

ONE

TWO

THREE

FOUR

FIVE

SIX

BURNING SECRETS

SEVEN

EIGHT

NINE

TEN

Broken Gems Series

CRACKED SAPPHIRE

CRUSHED RUBY

FRACTURED DIAMOND

SHATTERED AMETHYST

SPLINTERED EMERALD

SALVAGING MARIGOLD


River's End Rescues Series


COCKY SAVIOR

SOME REGRETS ARE FOREVER

SOME FEARS CAN CONTROL YOU

SOME LIES WILL HAUNT YOU

SOME QUESTIONS HAVE NO ANSWERS

SOME TRUTH CAN BE DISTORTED

SOME TRUST CAN BE REBUILT

SOME MISTAKES ARE UNFORGIVABLE


Candella Sisters' Heroes Series


LITTLE DOLLS

LITTLE HEARTS

LITTLE BALLERINA


Storybook Murders Series


NURSERY RHYME KILLER

FAIRYTALE KILLER

FABLE KILLER

Saving SEALs Series

SAVING RYDER

SAVING ERIC

SAVING OWEN

SAVING LOGAN

SAVING GRAYSON

SAVING CHARLIE

Prey Security Series

PROTECTING EAGLE

PROTECTING RAVEN

PROTECTING FALCON

PROTECTING SPARROW

PROTECTING HAWK

PROTECTING DOVE

Prey Security: Alpha Team Series

DEADLY RISK

LETHAL RISK

EXTREME RISK

FATAL RISK

COVERT RISK

SAVAGE RISK

Prey Security: Artemis Team Series

IVORY'S FIGHT

PEARL'S FIGHT

LACEY'S FIGHT

OPAL'S FIGHT


Prey Security: Bravo Team Series


VICIOUS SCARS

RUTHLESS SCARS


Christmas Romantic Suspense Series


CHRISTMAS HOSTAGE

CHRISTMAS CAPTIVE

CHRISTMAS VICTIM

YULETIDE PROTECTOR

YULETIDE GUARD

YULETIDE HERO

HOLIDAY GRIEF


Conquering Fear Series (Co-written with Amanda Siegrist)


DROWNING IN YOU

OUT OF THE DARKNESS

CLOSING IN

# About the Author

USA Today bestselling author Jane Blythe writes action-packed romantic suspense and military romance featuring protective heroes and heroines who are survivors. One of Jane's most popular series includes Prey Security, part of Susan Stoker's OPERATION ALPHA world! Writing in that world alongside authors such as Janie Crouch and Riley Edwards has been a blast, and she looks forward to bringing more books to this genre, both within and outside of Stoker's world. When Jane isn't binge-reading she's counting down to Christmas and adding to her 200+ teddy bear collection!

To connect and keep up to date please visit any of the following